"In Which Case" is a prequel to the stage disaster novel
"And Burnt The Topless Towers"

After the tragedy in the novel 'Theatre Wagon' John Mason has returned to the
world of major touring musicals, bruised and emotionally battered. But his
attempt to forget about what happened by burying himself in his work is
repeatedly thwarted by the complex backstage events on this show.

All the characters in this book are fictitious and any resemblance to any person
living or dead is purely co-incidental

The author, Cliff Dix, has worked in the entertainment industry
for over fifty years. His autobiographical reminiscences are
published in "Up The Fire Escape And Through The Kitchens"

To Ann. For putting up with it again!

IN WHICH CASE

Chapter 1

John Mason looked across the desk at his boss reclining in the big, comfortable, swivel chair. This theatre was grand and pretentious enough to boast a 'director's suite' for the use of visiting touring companies, and Levi Fischer was making full use of it.

The entrepreneur producer's body filled the well upholstered chair, and he leant back swinging it slightly from side to side as he paid full attention to lighting a cigar.

"Have one my boy," he said to John, waving toward the box on the desk between them.

John shook his head, saying "No thanks."

"You've earned it. The show's doing well. Of course we knew it would. It did well in London, now it's doing well for us." Levi seemed to think for a moment. "Mind you it's costing me a fortune."

John smiled inwardly. The old skinflint wasn't going to admit to the profits that had been rolling in over the past three months.

Behind Levi the expensively panelled room and heavy drapes reflected this provincial theatre's history of successes. A door, standing slightly open, hinted of the private dressing room beyond. A well stocked drinks cabinet to one side beckoned. John wondered whether he would be offered something from there. Perhaps it was a little too early in the morning.

John had been surprised at the summons to meet with Levi before coffee time on a weekday morning. Like most theatre people he, and his boss, didn't really believe in the day starting till at least lunchtime, but Levi had been most insistant. John assumed that that he was about to return to London, probably to set up another show business deal. It was a reasonable guess. The show was due to pull out of this venue after tomorrow's two performances and Levi didn't need to hang around watching his investment for tonight and the matinee and evening shows tomorrow. In fact his presence at the theatre at the tail end of a residence was slightly unusual. Levi was in no hurry to explain the purpose of this meeting.

"I've got no complaints," the producer went on. "No. You, and the company, of course, you're doing very well. And you know the show. What were you? Stage Director wasn't it on the West End run?"

John rubbed the scar on his arm, it was itching, and thought, 'You know full well I was. What are you trying to lead up to?'

Levi studied the end of his cigar, then tapped the ash off into an already nearly full glass ashtray on the desk.

"That's why I wanted you to run this tour for me. That's why I asked you to be the Company Manager. There's pretty much nothing you don't know about this show, and..." he paused significantly, "I want you to understand this my boy: I trust you. That's very important to me. I trust you."

Another pause, during which John wondered if he was about to be given the sack. He could think of no reason but had a fleeting moment of concern.

"I think what I'm going to tell you may be a bit of a surprise. It's unusual. But I'm sure it's in the best interests of everyone."

'Blast him, if he was going to sack me he might at least have given me a drink." John thought.

"I'm giving you an assistant." announced Levi, with the air of one who was presenting a tremendous gift.

John didn't quite know what to say. He'd never heard of a set up where the Company Manager had an assistant. It was an arrangement that was perfectly normal for Stage Managers, but an Assistant Company Manager?

"Are we talking about a trainee?" he queried, visualising an added workload nurse-maiding some youth on the first steps in theatrical management.

"Exactly. Well sort of. I want this assistant to take some of the stress out of it all for you. You are very valuable to me, John. I don't want you overworked."

John protested. In truth the requirements of the job were ideal for him, keeping at least part of his mind occupied most of his waking hours. The coming weekend, with the logistical organisation of up-rooting a major musical and transfering it across the country to another venue to re-open less than forty-eight hours after the Saturday night curtain fell was something he was anticipating keenly. It would take his mind off the 'other thing' for a few days. And when the slacker middle of the residency at the new venue came round there was always the local pubs and bars.

No. The present arrangement suited him as well as anything could be expected to. He didn't want an assistant, whether that person's presence lightened the load or made more work by forcing him to train them. It crossed his mind that he might not even like the new assistant. Why had Levi suddenly dropped this on him, without even talking it through first? They'd known each other for years, and, although he was Levi's employee, their meetings were usually more like chats between equals. Now some decision had been made without him being consulted, and he didn't like it. It puzzled him. Something didn't ring quite true, but he couldn't put his finger on what.

"I don't need an assistant, Levi. It's just going to confuse things. No-one's going to know who to refer to about what, or who's done what come to that."

"It's just to help you, John. I don't want to strain you any more than you have been. We all know about..." Levi broke off, seemingly embarrassed. "Well, we all know."

John wished people wouldn't keep bringing it up. But then he wished they'd be more open and talk about it. He wasn't going to forget her. Sometimes he wished he could have a conversation, just talk to someone about it. But he knew he wouldn't. It was too bitter, too personal, and still, for him, too recent, and he wasn't one to talk much about personal things.

They were interrupted as the director's suite 'secret' pass door, let into a side wall, and wall-papered to match the rest of the room, which allowed the occupant to get access to the back of the theatre's circle balcony, was abruptly opened, and an overall clad lady burst through dragging a vacuum cleaner.

"Sorry love. Didn't expect there to be anyone here this early. Shall I come back, or do you want me to leave it?"

"Leave it!" Levi snapped.

John smiled at the woman and made a shrugging gesture of apology for the other man's rudeness, but the cleaner was gone with a 'Well..!' and a faint odour of disinfectant and polish hanging in the air behind her as the door closed again.

"Don't these people ever knock?" he grumbled, before going on, "I want to help you, John. So you're having an assistant. Give them a separate office next to yours at the next venue and label it 'Assistant Company Manager' so there's no confusion, and John.." he gave him a strange look, "it's got to happen, so let the newcomer take some of the weight."

It was clearly a dismissal, so John got up and turned to leave the room by the door that led to the backstage world. As he reached it he looked back at Levi, who was studying the end of his cigar again.

"I don't like disrupting the established set-up," he said over his shoulder, "And I'm surprised at you taking on an extra salary unnecessarily."

Levi pointed the cigar at him, jabbing it for emphasis, saying "Don't you concern yourself about their salary, it's all taken care of and it won't appear in the show wages sheets."

John puzzled about this as he walked the corridors and staircases to descend from the top floor suite to the less pretentious dressing room levels below. After three flights of bare concrete steps, with a white stripe painted across the edge of each tread and with metal handrails bolted to the bare brick walls, he arrived at stage level, turning along the row of dressing rooms nearest to the stage itself. Here naturally were the best 'star' dressing rooms, and the doors he passed bore the names of the principals in the show. Further along the last two doors on the sides of this particular passage were labelled 'Stage Mangement' and then 'Company Manager'.

He paused by the door to his own room and looked back along the brick alley. It was like so many backstage areas, basic and functional. This one had had its brickwork painted in gloss paint at some time; the bottom half a dark maroon and the upper half of the wall in cream. The show's own labelling of the doors was a minor bit of showiness on John's part, dispensing with the usual hand written label or card stuck to each door he had arranged for quantities of cards with the show logo and the actor or actresses name to be printed before the tour started. Thus, looking along the corridor, you saw a smart series of name-plates. It was a mere petty-cash item, but bolstered the egos of his company. 'Assistant Company Manager' hand written on a card was going to look very tatty.

He let himself into his own room and flopped on a chair in front of the dressing table shelf that was acting as a desk, shoving his typewriter to one side to lean on his elbows and stare at his own reflection in the light-bulb surrounded mirror.

'Now what,' he asked himself, 'is really going on with this new 'assistant'?'

* * *

Upstairs the door to the suite's private dressing room opened more fully. Levi swivelled in the chair to look at the figure that emerged.

"Is that what you wanted of me?" he asked.

"Excellent. Thank you for your co-operation Mr Fischer."

"Make sure you tell your people that I don't like deceiving my best man."

"Just a little white lie."

Levi grunted and scowled. His cigar had gone out.

Chapter 2

A purposeful bustling was in the air backstage the next day. It was Saturday, and, apart from the usual extra work involved in a matinee and evening performance, this Saturday would see the whole show moved from its present home of some five weeks to another venue nearly a hundred miles away.

Overnight the scenery, costumes, props, musical instruments, lighting and sound equipment and the cast and crew would transfer to a new home for a month and a half long run in the latest city on the tour. By Monday night all would be re-assembled and ready for the audience in this new location to see exactly the same show as tonight's audience would see.

There was no panic at this approaching task. There would be just a quicker packing and clearing at the end of the evening performance. Wardrobe staff would hang costumes in travelling boxes, instead of loading them into washing machines or tidying them on dressing room rails once each specific garment had appeared for the last time. ASMs would do the same with props, and there would even be some stealthy dismantling of scenic items as they were finished with, ready for loading into the waiting articulated lorries.

The new assistant company manager arrived about lunchtime. John managed to conceal his surprise when she came and introduced herself to him. Nothing had been said, and he had expected a man.

She was a rather athletic looking woman in her mid thirties, wearing a mannish dark suit which looked to John to be too clean and well pressed to have spent much time in the backstage world. John's own long established image of being rather smart among his peers, always favouring collar and tie over tee shirts and jeans, looked likely to be put in the shade.

He took a quick look at his watch and said, "Come on, let's go and have a drink and get something to eat, and you can tell me all about yourself."

The pub near the stage door was quite crowded. Members of both cast and crew, who made up the bulk of the clientelle, greeted John as he and the newcomer squeezed their way to the bar. A couple of the lorry drivers had already arrived, and manoeuvered their trucks into position by the theatre's loading bay ready for the get-out. John greeted them cheerfully, but didn't introduce the new girl.

It was some time before the two of them were wedged in a corner with ploughmans' lunches and drinks; a Britvic orange for her, and a pint and a whisky chaser for him.

Her name was Moira. He was stunned when he asked about previous jobs to be told she'd never done this sort of thing before, and, when he pressed her, to discover that her only background in show business was some work with an amateur company when she was in her teens. His attitude hardened as she revealed more, or perhaps, in truth, less of her stage experience, and he sat mentally rehearsing what he would be saying to Levi when he rang him on Monday. He knew it would not be till Monday, for, despite the nature of the business, Levi's office was habitually resolutely closed from Friday night to Monday morning.

His mind ran ahead to the next venue. The Royal was one of those great houses which he welcomed taking shows into. He knew many of the staff. He made a decision. If Levi wanted to believe that this woman was being useful and taking some of John's workload he would have to give her some tasks.

The house manager, Jimmy, at the Royal was an old friend of John's. He would ring him during the matinee this afternoon and tell him about the situation. If he gave her over to Jimmy she could be set to dealing with paperwork about posters and programme sales that between them they could keep her occupied with for days.

He swigged his pint.

The youngeest wardrobe assistant passed by saying 'Hello' and smiling at John.

Moira asked, "Who's she?" almost suspiciously.

"Lucy Gainsborough, one of the wardrobe staff. Nice girl," he said, his mind on what else he could occupy Moira with.

The new assistant watched Lucy vanishing into the crowd with an unfathomable look.

"Have you met her before?" John asked. If Moira had been a member of the small world of touring theatre backstage staff it would have been highly likely, but somehow John couldn't see how that could be with someone so evidently outside the usual clique.

"Gainsborough." a pause, "No, not met..." and then Moira stopped and changed the subject, asking about timings and the arrangements in the next city. Her naivety showed with this more and more, as she used layman's language instead of theatre jargon, and asked a few questions that no-one would have needed to if they'd ever worked on a show.

Deciding that he had better educate her as much as possible he finished his meal and drinks and took her to the box office to arrange a comp ticket for her to watch the matinee of this show she clearly knew nothing about. Once he had armed her with a house seat he pointed her in the general direction of the circle and left her to make his way backstage, saying "Watch the show carefully," before he vanished.

Not very much later the last matinee performance of "Chuzzlewit" in this particular theatre began.

There wasn't much work for John during a performance, and he sat in the company office sifting routine paperwork and filling in the details of the box office returns for the past twenty-four hours in the company's ledger.

The familiar music could be heard over the show relay system speaker in his room. This touring version had mostly a different cast, though a few of the original people had retained their parts, and this made the show he could hear from the speaker infuriatingly familiar but just slightly wrong to his ears. It was, he decided, like hearing a cover version of a well known song, well remembered but with unaccostomed cadences. For a while he day-dreamed about the original London run of the show, when he had been stage director, and he and Melanie had been married. It wasn't Melanie's face he saw if he closed his eyes, however. A spasm of grief brought him back to the present day, and he opened the cupboard under the dressing table, pulled out a three quarters empty bottle of whisky, and poured a generous measure into a china mug.

The performance carried on, and John spent the time on the mountain of paperwork that a major touring show generates.

Quite late in act two a brief knock on the door hearalded his stage manager who stuck his head round the door and announced, "The third truck's arrived. It's your mate Reg."

"Thanks Frank," John answered, "I'll come out and see him in a minute."

"He's gone round to the café near the box office,"

"OK. No surprise there then. I'll be there soon."

He finished the figures he had been filling in on a spreadsheet, stretched, and went out of the stage door, along the narrow and slightly grimy, dank passage that led to the street.

'Why are all stage doors hidden in unsalubrious alleyways?' he mused, as he pushed open the door of the steamy café, spotting Reg at a table with his nose buried in a large mug of tea.

"Hi Reg."

Reg looked up, a big man, unshaven from too many nights away from conventional bed and board. He spent much of his time in the cab of his truck.

"John!" He lowered the mug, and leant to one side to allow the waitress, who had just appeared, to place a large 'all day breakfast' in front of him. It seemed to John that the meal had been served with extra everything.

"Do you want to eat with me?"

The waitress looked fondly and enquiringly at John.

"All right, yes. An all day... but without the extras, and tea please." he said to her.

She nodded, still smiling at John, who had been something of a favourite regular in the café for over a month now, and headed off towards the counter.

John sat down opposite Reg.

"Tell me the worst about tonight then." said the truck driver, digging into his meal with gusto.

"I think you know. It won't come down till after ten-thirty. Wardrobe will probably be ready soon after that, so we can fling that on the first truck as usual, but it's the regular hold up with electrics and sound for the rest of that load. We'll probably have at least the bulk of the next truck packed before anything with plugs on emerges. You know the score. I take it you are tail end Charlie as usual?"

"Always." he shovelled up some chips. "Someone has to follow behind to round up the stragglers."

John's food arrived and he busied himself adding sugar to the mug of tea. Reg asked,

"Do you want a lift with me tonight or are you sorted with some luxury transport?"

"A lift would be good if you don't mind."

"Nah, glad of the company. Though I know you, you'll sleep all the way."

They ate in companionable silence for a while, then through the windows John could see the pavements suddenly filling up.

"The matinee's come down." he said. He looked at his watch, as if there was any real doubt about the time, and said, "Punctual."

By the time he'd finished eating, and Reg, still demolishing the contents of his piled plate, had ordered another mug of tea, the streets were beginning to clear. The café door, which had been opening and shutting a lot, opened again to reveal Moira peering through and clearly looking for John. With recognition, and what might possibly have been relief at finding him, she came over and sat with the two men. Reg looked at John inquiringly.

"This is my new assistant, Moira. Moira, Reg. Reg is the lead truck driver."

"Except I'm never in the lead, I'm always last." Reg said holding out a hand, which engulfed Moira's as they shook.

"Moira only joined us today, she's been watching the matinee."

Reg nodded, still eating.

"And what did you learn from watching the show?" John asked the newcomer.

"I knew some of the tunes I suppose." she said.

"Did you get the sequence of the scene changes and how it works?"

"Well...."

'Oh god,' John thought, 'she's got no idea of what we are supposed to be doing.' Aloud he said, "Get something to eat. I want you to watch from the wings tonight."

"Why?" she challenged, "I've seen it now."

"Because you need to know the show inside out if you are to be some sort of help. We sometimes have to make changes to suit a new venue and any change has a knock-on effect. You have to know it well to predict those," he explained, trying to be patient.

She looked at the table and saw that they'd now both finished and said, "OK. I'll see you later."

"By the half," he told her. She looked a bit blank.

"Thirty-five minutes before curtain up." he told her, a little exasperated.

"Whatever," she said, with a disinterested shrug.

She left, and Reg watched the door close before saying, "Assistant?"

"That's what the big bosses tell me."

"So who's she sleeping with then? 'Cos she's certainly no practical use to you or anyone else, far too green... and I don't think she's your type."

"I just don't know. I'm going to have words with Levi on Monday"

"Do that, John. The last thing you need is having to do everything twice to check on what she's mucked up. Help is one thing, and just maybe you should have it, but a raw trainee is different."

John shrugged. "Perhaps she's someone's relative." He looked into his mug and found it was empty.

Later he was standing in the company office fuming slightly. He glanced at his watch. The DSM had called 'Ladies and gentlement this is your half hour call, half an hour please', but there was no sign of Moira. It annoyed him. Five minutes after 'the half' she arrived.

"You're late," he snapped more bluntly than he intended.

She looked surprised, checked her watch, and said, "No I'm not, it's exactly half an hour before the start."

John gave a sigh of wearied patience explaining to her, "The half is thirty-five minutes before the start, the five minute call is ten minutes before, and 'beginners' is five minutes before. That's to allow five minutes from the beginners call for everyone to be in position. I told you thirty-five minutes before curtain up."

"Well I didn't know about your weird system."

His attitude hardened at the standard theatre system being called 'weird' by this evident outsider. To him the customs, traditions and routines of the entertainment world were second nature and sacrosanct.

"There seem to be a lot of things you don't know. So keep your eyes and ears open and please try to learn." He led her out into the corridor. "Come on, we'll watch the first half from the wings."

But as the show went on he became increasingly sure that the woman was not learning anything. Twice he had to motion her to step aside, as some scenic piece was moved in their direction. Eventually a moment came when the entire chorus was rushing toward an exit she was standing in. He put a hand on her shoulder to pull her back out of the way, and was startled when she spun round adopting an aggressive, defensive stance towards him. Her hands were raised as if to attack him. In the darkness of the wings he was momentarily frightened of her. It was a sensation he greatly disliked. It annoyed him that this stranger could come into this world, his world, a world where he had spent a working lifetime feeling safe and comfortable, and make the atmosphere unpleasant for him in an instant. 'Perhaps she doesn't like being touched,' he thought, 'but that reaction was over the top.' The chorus swept past them in the gloom, wide Victorian dresses brushing against the minor obstruction that they were causing as the orchestra played the link that covered a scene change that was simultaneously taking place. The show, he was delighted to observe, ploughed on unaffected by the presence of this outsider he was supposed to be training.

By the interval John was both saddened and aggravated. He began to realise that he, and his fellow theatre people, had a whole lifetime of instinctive background to draw on. Even the most callow casual stage hand would have some general concept after the first week or two of employment in any venue. True, he thought, the standard of their expertise would be strongly influenced by the common practices of the venue they started in, but there was a shared knowledge and expectation running through the industry.

He took Moira away from the Act one finale, and the interval scene change that would follow the fall of the curtain at this half way point, and led her to his office.

"Now," he said, once the door had closed behind them, the usual interval babble in the corridors was shut out and he had turned down the volume on the show relay speaker on the wall of the room, which was broadcasting the sound of an audience, "do you understand how it all fits together now you've seen it from out-front and from the wings?"

She looked at him solemnly. He had a feeling that she resented being questioned, but he didn't care any more. He needed to be assured that some small spark of insight into the whole mass of interlocking human and mechanical parts that went to make up a major musical show was growing in her mind. Perhaps it wouldn't matter if she was a complete novice if she was keen to learn.

She shrugged.

"Look," he said, "if you're supposed to be helping me you have to know at least the basics. I tell you what, take this," he rummaged desperately on the dressing table shelf and found a clipboard and some lists. Thumbing through the close typed lists he selected a few and clipped them to the board. He handed her this and a pencil. "..and check this stuff off on the list as it gets loaded when the show is over."

He'd deliberately selected the list of items travelling in the trucks for the orchestra, basically the instruments that were too big, or awkward, for their owners to wish take them in their own cars, He'd picked this, as the orchestra fixer was known to be fastidious about ensuring that everything got loaded, so her checking would be totally superfluous. In any case the orchestra pit would be the subject of an 'idiot check' before the doors shut, and musicians were thorough with packing their particular items.

She took the list from him reluctantly he thought.

Despairingly he said, "You don't really want to do this do you?"

"I've been given my orders and I'll carry them out, so don't worry."

"Orders from me, or orders from Levi?"

"Does it matter? I've been told to assist you."

"I don't understand at all. Who's told you to help me? And why?" John demanded.

"I'm told you need help. I'm it." she told him.

The end-of-interval calls interrupted this unsatisfactory conversation.

"Just check the orchestra's gear gets loaded," he instructed. And he left her standing in his office and made off through the passageways to escape via the pass door to front of house to watch the second half start.

He'd always liked the act two opening. Even the minor changes wrought on the show by reviving it, after a gap, with a mostly new cast hadn't changed his feeling for this part. The staging, dance routine and musical number all appealed to him, yet that evening it was soured for him by this woman's attitude, lack of theatrical background, and having been parachuted onto him against his will for reasons he did not understand. He stood in an alcove along the wall of the stalls, well out of the way of audience view, and watched the show. His show, he thought; for out here on the road everything involving the production was his responsibility. He leant back against the deep burgundy wallpaper, its flock worn a bit threadbare in places by the traffic of hundreds of bodies, willing himself to unwind and let the show soothe him. He had, he knew, a few hectic and potentially stressful days ahead as the show pulled out of here, drove across the country, and was re-assembled in the next venue. He had no real concern about the practicalities. Long experience meant that he was confident in his own ability, and he knew his crew would cope with any unforseen problems. Not that he expected the Royal to present any. But a change of venue always produced slight variations in backstage routine. The simplest change of layout meant that you took more or fewer paces to reach a dressing room, that you turned left or right at some corridor junction, that the bar was further away... He thought about the bar. Was it time for a last drink in the front of house bar here? No. He disciplined himself reluctantly in readiness for the get-out tonight.

The get-out came soon enough. The finale and curtain calls, to another standing ovation, gave way to the labour of dismantling and removing the show from the bleakly lit and rapidly emptying stage and auditorium. The audience were safely back in their various homes long before the waiting trucks were loaded and ready to roll off towards the Royal.

Just as John had predicted the wardrobe department was winning the race, and cases, skips and hanging rails all disappeared into a waiting truck along with the washing machines and driers, irons and ironing boards that the show carried. The young wardrobe girl smiled at John as she passed him, wheeling a case full of shoes. He grinned back, "Keep at it, Lucy."

"Oh I will...Family in the next city!" she panted back at him, breathlessly.

"I didn't know that," he shouted after her, but against the bedlam of the mostly steel scenic parts being taken apart he wasn't sure if she heard. He shrugged. There were lots of things he didn't know about her. Come to think of it there were lots of things he didn't know about many of his company. He realised this was unusual for him. Ever since he had assumed the management roles on a variety of shows he had usually known all about everyone. It was not nosiness, it was sound management policy. The more you knew the less likely unpleasant surprises would creep up and bite you. Perhaps, he thought, he hadn't been paying enough attention to this touring version of 'Chuzzlewit'. He mentally resolved to remedy this in the next city, and not just because he felt he would like to know more about Lucy. It wasn't a feeling he had had for a long time, certainly not since the accident. He knew he would never be over it. In some ways he didn't actually want to get over it. But maybe, just maybe, he should stop hiding away from any new relationships, and Lucy was a friendly girl.

"Mind your back!"

A shout from a member of the house crew, struggling under the weight of one of the show's bigger bits of set, brought him back to the present."

He muttered 'sorry' and leapt aside. It reminded him of Moira's faux-pas earlier. He felt some guilt. 'Pay attention to the show,' he told himself.

The get-out and loading continued. Somewhere below the stage, in an area backing onto the orchestra pit, Moira was watching the musicians packing instruments and music scores into cases. She didn't entirely understand the ownership, contents or uses of the cases, but tried to keep track of what was going on. In essence the larger items were going to the trucks, and members of the house crew working the get-out kept appearing and wheeling or carrying these away.

She held a clip-board in her hand, but couldn't decide what, if any, notes to make. Nor could she really understand the detailled lists of equipment that she was supposed to be checking. Some instruments she could recognise, though like most lay people she was at a loss over the differences between a violin and a viola or an alto or tenor sax. She was supposed to be noting what was in the cases, but a realisation of the enormity, even the impossibility, of that task was dawning on her. There had to be another way of checking on the contents of the, quite literally hundreds, of boxes, cases and crates that a show of this scale transported each time it moved venue she thought. The musicians and crew passed and repassed, pushing past her without comment in the furious haste of the get-out.

On stage John was similarly surveying the get-out operation, though in his case with understanding and knowledge. It was not really any different to a venue to venue move of any major show. John's approach was to allow each crew member to take responsibility for the safe stowage of the parts that concerned them, only intervening when the demands of truck loading or another department's requirements might not be high on a particular section's agenda. A quiet word would solve any hold-up caused. But there would not be any hold ups on this evening he knew. The show had moved before, and snags had long been ironed out, besides this was a very experienced crew. Well apart from that Moira woman he thought.

The get-out continued into the early hours. The stage emptied. The lorries filled.

"Come on, if you're hitching a lift with me, some of us need to be on the road." Reg's voice nagged John into cutting short the quiet checking of the dark corners of the, now empty, stage and his peering up into the yawning grid space to make sure nothing remained hanging there.

"Yes, just coming," John shouted back.

With a series of handshakes and goodbyes, and 'see you again's he left the theatre, going out to the waiting lorry. He threw his bag in through the open passenger door, seized the grab handle, and swung himself up into the cab. He slammed the door. The theatre's resident stage manager had a brief glimpse of the haulage company's telephone number glinting in the reflected street-light on the highly polished bodywork as the door closed, of John reaching over his shoulder for the seatbelt, and half waving in farewell, as the truck rolled forward and away from the loading bay.

Reg drove the lorry quickly and confidently through the deserted streets to the motorway juction, joining the nearly empty carriageway and heading towards the next venue.

He and John said little till the truck was on the main road and

rolling steadily toward their destination. When they were well
under way Reg said, "Well, how did your new 'assistant' get on?"

John grunted. "I got her out of my hair. I sent her down to the
orchestra pit. That lot won't have let her interfere, and don't need
any help from anyone else in packing their gear. I did a quick
idiot check, but they've never been known to lose so much as a
drumstick."

"Very clever. Where are you sending her while the get-in
happens?"

"I thought about out front, with sound or LX. The noise boys and
the sparks all talk a completely foreign language, she'll either give
up and leave us, or become totally bogged down in trying to
follow it all."

"You are a devious sod aren't you?"

"I do my best." John paused. "of course if you want her with you
off-loading..."

Reg made a rude noise.

"OK, OK. It was just an idea,"

"Ideas like that I can do without." and then he added, "Anyway
that only solves a couple of days of get-in. What the hell are you
going to do with her then?"

"Ah, I've got an idea about that. You see I don't think I know the
company very well, well not like I knew the original company..."

"Yes, we all know what knowing them well led to!"

"Oh shut-up, that's not what I meant, and you know it!"

"Sorry, touched a nerve."

"No. Well not really. Anyway I figure if I've got to go round with this thing for the foreseeable future I'd better know the cast... and crew if it comes to that, rather better. So I'm going to tour the dressing rooms systematically and do a somewhat belated 'meet and greet'.

"You're just hoping to get bought drinks."

"Well there is that."

"So that aside, how does this solve the assistant problem?"

John sighed. "It doesn't completely, but she'll either trail round with me, which if there are other people about means someone else can talk to her, or I can leave her in the company office on the excuse of someone 'minding the shop'."

"I hope she doesn't 'mind it' into too much of a muddle."

"So do I," said John, "So do I." and they lapsed into silence as the miles rolled by.

Despite a stop at an all-night roadside café they made good time. John dozed in the passenger seat and awoke to the streets of the next city slipping past as Reg jockied his way to the new venue in the cold light of early day.

Soon they were going along the road that led to the venue. First they caught a glimpse of the show's publicity, but as they got closer the opposite theatre's frontage and posters caught John's attention. It was an ugly cream tiled frontage reminiscent of a sixties cinema, the posters and signs promoting 'All Invited To A Murder'. He had known the show would be there. He was unsurprised to see the strident billing 'Starring Laurence Drover' but a little taken aback to see 'Nicole Wade' in tiny letters among the supporting cast. He hadn't thought her role was big enough to warrant any billing from what he had heard on the grapevine.

Reg might have been leaning forward to watch the near side of the lorry as he came toward the turn to the theatre's loading doors, but somehow John suspected that he was really watching his passenger's face. This assumption was confirmed when Reg, swinging the wheel energetically to pull skillfully into a position by the dock doors at the side of the grander theatre, nodded at the posters and said, "Some of your old cast aren't they?"

John knew that Reg wasn't really asking a question, that he knew full well the answer. He also guessed that he'd known these players from the past were appearing at the venue opposite, in the same street. Reg might have been exclusively a truck driver, but he was an assiduous reader of 'The Stage', and his almost obsessive interst in 'show-biz' explained his broad knowledge of the ways of the industry.

"Yes," John answered him, slowly, "some of an old cast." He stopped there, but he knew that Reg had already worked out which show, and knew why it might affect him. He wasn't sure how he was going to react to what he suspected would be an unavoidable meeting with his two former cast members at some point during the show's stay here.

The thoughts were interrupted anyway as the lorry finally stopped amid some hissing of air brakes, and the process of off-loading and getting the show in was about to start. He climbed out of the cab, thanking Reg for the ride, and, grabbing his bag, headed into the building via the stage door with a brief glance along the road to the junction, where the 'All Invited To A Murder' billing was just visible.

Despite the early hour there were cheery 'good mornings' from the stage-door keeper and those members of the resident crew who recognised him from previous visits with other touring shows. John soon immersed himself in the business of starting the unloading of the trucks, allocating the dressing rooms and so on. He'd had time to do this, take a quick shower and grab tea and a bacon roll from the nearby cafe long before Moira put in an appearance.

She arrived when the first truck was already half unloaded. Following the door-keeper's directions she found her way to the room John had earmarked as the Company Office. She stood in the doorway with a suitcase, shoulder bag and thick coat over her arm. She managed to give an impression of a refugee he thought. Confusion, bewilderment and uncertainty seemed etched on her face. Normally John's reaction to someone looking a bit lost and forlorn would have been one of sympathy, Somehow Moira didn't elicit that response in him. Clearly she was not used to this sort of life. He wondered why she hadn't put her suitcase on the lorry with the rest of the cast and crew baggage. Most of them only travelled with an overnight bag in their own car or on the train. Presumably she didn't know that routine, and no-one had told her.

"Hello," he said, "Good journey?"

"It was further than I thought," she told him. "I'll dump my bags in here shall I?"

"Have you sorted out your digs yet?" He wasn't too keen on the office becoming a dumping ground, although his own luggage would doubtless appear soon.

"No," she replied, "not yet."

"I suggest you have a look at the list at the stage door and go and book in somewhere first, then come back and join in the fun. Stage management has the off-loading under control and we won't be seeing too much set building till it's off the trucks. But come straight back, I thought you might want to shadow the LX side of things."

"LX?"

"Electrics.. lighting.." he paused frustrated again, "The guys with all those flight cases."

"Ah! Yes, that might be good. I'll be back soon." And grappling with her bags she turned in the door and was gone again.

'Now why would she suddenly become interested because I said 'flight cases'?' he mused.

Time flew by, as it always does when there's a lot of work to be done. It was lunchtime before John gave Moira any further thought. Some gear was hanging from the flying bars, Odd parts of the scenery had vanished to the grid. A couple of the major scenic trucks were part-way through construction. By a mutual agreement the resident and touring crews called a halt and made off to the local pub for lunch. John followed, calling in at the hotel he had booked to check in before making his way to the crowded bar.

The two crews were well into their drinks and their ploughmans lunches or pies. John was pleased to see that they had mingled quite a lot. If there were separations it looked as though they were departmental rather than a residents-touring crew split. Certainly the electrics deprtment of the venue was deep in conversation with the touring electrics crew he had told Moira to shadow, and as he passed them he could tell that the conversation was social rather than a discussion about technical requirements for the show. Similar socialising seemed to be going on elsewhere. He looked about and Lucy caught his eye. She indicated a rare empty seat near her, and he gave her a thumbs up sign, gave a questioning mime of drinking to which she responded 'no thanks' holding up a nearly full glass, and made toward the bar. Once served, and clutching a packet of crisps and a double whisky, he joined the wardrobe girl at her table. He realised he didn't know any of the others she was with. Maybe they were members of the Royal's crew.

They were not.

Lucy introduced them. He didn't really catch the names, but he gathered that they were her family and that they mostly lived in the city. Lucy was pleased and excited to be spending a few weeks of the tour in her home town, where she could see her relatives and, probably, meet up with some old friends. John did gather that one of the younger men was her brother, and that he ran a launderette not very far from the theatre.

There were handshakes all round, and John ate his crisps and knocked back his whisky just in time to be aware of the crews getting up and starting to make their way back to work.

Back in the Royal John had a few technical discussions with Frank, the show's stage manager, which mostly concerned minor variations in layout caused by the move from venue to venue, before going back to the company office. There he set up his camp for the coming weeks and unpacked the dressing room door labels that he had printed off in advance at the last theatre.

The top one didn't concern 'Chuzzlewit's company at all, and was printed as 'Mollie's Garden Company Office'. He stuck this on the door next to his own. He added a second label to the door saying 'Chuzzlewit Assistant Company Manager'. 'Make her share', he thought. Anyway she might learn something from being thrown in with another show as well. He went in and laid the next three labels on the dressing table. Each said 'Mollie's Garden'

'Mollie's Garden' was the title of a popular series of childrens' cartoon books, which had been adapted for television and recently been turned into a stage show and this was now touring the country. The childrens' show seemed to have started following 'Chuzzlewit' round the circuit, playing underneath it. This meant that for three of weeks of 'Chuzzlewit's residency they would share the venue with 'Mollie's Garden', who would play matinees while 'Chuzzlewit' played evenings.

With the rest of the labels in his hand he toured the backstage passages, stopping at each dressing room and labelling it with the allocated performer's name, or names in the case of more minor roles. He came across a few company members in his travels, mainly wardrobe staff and ASMs, who were similarly distributing to the rooms, copies of the dressing room allocations clutched for consultation as they went. Costumes, personal props and the like would all await the cast when they took up residence. By arrangement the dressing rooms were all unlocked ready, the cast would pick up keys from the stage door. John took the opportunity to glance into a few to make sure that they were up to standard, though he knew The Royal, and its good reputation. The rooms were rather uniform in décor and fittings, though a few of the ones nearer the stage had en-suite facilities and in two cases a sitting room and a dressing room. These had been allocated to the stars of the show.

The passageways were all finished in deep coloured panel-work below, with light cream upper walls. The colour of the lower panels gave a clue to which floor you were on, as the panels were different for each floor. As the dressing room block had been built up of six superficially identical floors, aside from minor variations due to extra access doors at stage level and room for the stage door entrance at the level below, the colour code ran through the spectrum starting with a theatrical red at stage door and street level through to a dark violet on the top floor which was up at the level of the access to the theatre's fly tower.

The company office was on stage level, so the corridors were a rich orange.

The interior décor of the dressing rooms was, however, the same throughout the building, a wallpaper in vertical stripes of shades of grey, backing the varnished wood dressing tables shelves and mirrors, making a slightly cold feel.

The Royal had had a long overdue backstage refurbishment a couple of years previously, but already, he noticed, the grey striped carpets showed signs of wear at doorways and the panelled lower parts of the walls in the passages displayed horizontal scratches where wardrobe rails and skips had scuffed the paintwork at corners and darker patches at about chest height on the wallpaper corners at the entrance to each staircase showing the passing of countless hands over the weeks and months.

The Royal was still, for all this, smart and welcoming by comparison to many venues on the circuit.

He checked on a couple of the shower and toilet rooms at random as he went round, finding them clean and well maintained as he had guessed they would be. The showers ran hot quite quickly when he checked, despite what must have been enormous lengths of plumbing between tanks and outlets. John was pleased on behalf of his cast.

The checking and labelling he was doing might normally have been a task given to an ASM, but he liked to see for himself. He was always fastidious in caring for his company and this personal tour of a new venue ensured that there were no unexpected problems when the cast arrived.

He had gone up each level using the stairs. He felt he had earned the ride down in the lift. When he stepped out into the orange corridor at stage level he almost collided with Moira. She was exactly outside the lift doors and staring along the length of the passage with her back to him.

"Hello, I thought you were with electrics." he said.

"I was. I am. I just came to see... Doesn't matter." she told him, turned and headed towards the auditorium.

John wondered what she had been doing. There was something almost shady or suspicious about her.

By the evening 'Chuzzlewit' had settled itself into its new home. The stage was dark as electrics focussed and plotted positions for the moving fixtures in the rig. It was not completely quiet because the sound department was testing its gear, but the main part of the crew had left, only a couple of men remaining to do any scene changes that lighting might need.

John had dropped his baggage at his hotel, which was very close by, but had foregone the hotel's evening meal, settling for a quick 'pie and a pint' in the pub. Now he was in the stage management dressing room with Frank and Tania, the DSM, sitting at the room's make-up table checking a few adjustments to cues that the slight change of layout moving to The Royal had required.

Moira found them.

"How's electrics getting on?" he asked her. He knew exactly how they were getting on from what he could hear on the room's show relay speaker, but he thought he had better pretend Moira had some use, even if he was finding it hard going to keep her occupied.

"Er, I think they're all right."

Frank, who had also been half following progress by listening to the backstage speaker and who had no interest in trying to pretend that Moira was any use to them at all, said, "Three quarters of the way through Act one... they're usually a bit further on than that by now."

"Yes, but they should still be done by eleven, so we won't run into another overtime call."

"Just a tech and dress tomorrow."

Chapter 3

He was early to the venue on the Monday morning, ready for the routine technical run through which would familiarise the theatre's resident crew with the show, and the afternoon's dress rehearsal. Once these were over 'Chuzzlewit' would settle into it's month and a half long run at the Royal.

John had discovered that he would not be able to question Levi about the imposition of Moira on the show, as the entrepreneur had, slightly unusually, failed to come to this change of venue. There was a rumour of some dispute in one of the costal venues that Levi had a show running at. It was annoying to John, meaning that the confrontation would be delayed, probably for several weeks, as Levi rarely visited a show after its get-in weekend. John supposed that he should take comfort from the implication that he was trusted to manage everything, but as he personally never had any real doubt on that score the implicit compliment was wasted.

Early though he was some departments had already started work, Noticeably the theatre's maintenance men were coming and going in the backstage areas on some mysterious mission of their own. From the touring company he saw that wardrobe, still with mountains of washing drying and ironing to deal with before the afternoon dress rehearsal, were systematically visiting dressing rooms and distributing those costumes that were ready.

As he came out of the lift at stage level and turned toward the company office he passed Lucy heading outward, clutching a huge box of soap-powder and a bundle of garments zipped into a bag. He nodded and smiled at her and as he fumbled with the key in the company office door, looked back in time to see her shuffling round Moira in the confines of the passageway. Whether Moira's clearly antagonistic expression was due to their having to squeeze past each other owing to Lucy's burdens, or some antipathy toward the girl he wasn't sure, but his own attitude to Moira hardened further in defence of the young wardrobe assistant.

He deliberately bit his tongue and didn't comment on the incident when, a few moments later, Moira joined him in the office. They exchanged rather cold 'good morning's and he sent her off to hang around with the sound department, hoping that this would keep the woman away from him for the rest of the day.

As the layout at this theatre meant that anyone heading to wardrobe passed back and forth outside his office door he found himself becoming increasingly aware of the activities of that department, and of Lucy. He scolded himself privately for not having had more detailed knowledge of their tasks previously. He knew of the constant cleaning and maintenance, if only because of the regular bills from the detergent manufacturer that the show bought from. They got a cheap deal for including the brand name in the programme in a line that read 'wardrobe care by...'. None the less the monthly bill appeared in front of him to be passed for payment. Thinking about it he was hardly surprised at the size of the box of powder Lucy had been carrying, given the quantities involved. With his door open, as was his usual habit when he was in the room, he noticed her return from her early morning mission, and then leave again a couple of hours later, coming back with the zipped bag, presumably with the cleaned costumes in it.

The show carried its own washing machines, but bulkier items, and given the period dress there were many, often didn't fit the small row of almost domestic washers touring with them, so there was some reliance on the nearest local launderette. He wondered if she was using her brother's company. Probably, he thought.

As the morning wore on he began to regret the siting of the office in view of the persistant traffic outside the door. Seeking a break he went off to the stage door to collect the plug-in phone for the office. He should have picked this up yesterday, but it hadn't seemed urgent on a Sunday. Dangling the instrument by its rest, with the cable curled up in the same hand, he returned to the office, plugged it in to the wall socket, listened briefly to the dial tone, hung up and went along to wardrobe to check up on them.

Visiting wardrobe at some point during a residency wasn't that rare, he sometimes used the washing facilities for his own clothes, as did almost everyone else in the company, or for a quick cup of tea or coffee, but the couple of days of get-in didn't usually see him in that area.

He was greeted by a steamy room, made noisy by one of the machines being in the process of spinning, where two women, Lucy was out on another errand, were ironing parts of costumes and hanging them on hangers on rails to be distributed. Clipboards with lists of names and garments lay around with various columns of boxes ticked.

"It's no use you coming here wanting to scrounge a cup of coffee when we're busy love," yelled Brenda, the head wardrobe mistress, with a cheery wave across the room.

"You know I wouldn't do that," he replied, "though if the kettle's on...."

"I'll do it," shouted Alice, her assistant, from near the vibrating machine. She filled the kettle at one of the sinks and plugged it in next to a tray of coffee jars, sugar packets and mugs.

"Now I feel guilty.

"So you should," Brenda laughed.

"I only dropped by to see that you were all OK and had got everything you needed."

"More time would be nice. Can you postpone first night here?"

"What? Ruin your reputation for always being ready before everyone else? I don't think you mean that." He was shouting over the spin cycle, which chose that exact moment to finish with a winding down noise which meant his response was far too loud.

"Now he's shouting at us Alice," said Brenda, in a normal voice, "What have we done wrong now?"

"I assume everything is fine then."

"Thanks, yes, we're OK."

"You did know Lucy's got relatives locally didn't you?" Alice cut in on her boss's reply to John.

"Yes. I gather he owns a launderette."

"Seems so, We're using him for the bulky stuff while we're here, just so you know."

"I thought you probably would if he's nearby. Are we getting any discount?"

"Honestly, John, I didn't like to ask for it. I think, reading between the lines, that the poor bloke is struggling a bit. It's her brother you know," Brenda told him.

Alice was making coffees for them all.

"That's all right. I wouldn't want to push it, especially if money's tight for him. Oh, thank you Alice."

"White with three. That's right for coffee isn't it?"

"Brilliant. Can you really remember everyone's preferences in the company?"

"When the entire company use you as a backstage café you get to remember. Especially the ones who're forever on the beg." Brenda winked at him so he knew she didn't mean it, turned, and began unloading the machine.

"Anyway," John said to Alice, "didn't you used to be in some memory act, or was it magic?"

"Actually he was a stage pickpocket. I was the distraction, you know, sparkly costume.. lots of leg. I used to hold a tray that he put the things he had lifted from the punters' pockets on. Though it wasn't often from pockets, it was things like wrist watches and cufflinks mostly."

"Why did you give it up?" John sipped his tea.

"The cabaret world was dying out, killed off by discos. Anyway I wasn't really the right shape any more."

There wasn't much he could say in answer to that and John was sure he was holding them up, so he left, saying "Thanks, I'll bring the cup back." and went back to his room, As he got there the phone he had just plugged in was ringing. He answered it to find it was Levi calling in from the coast.

"You've got a phone at last my boy. How difficult should it be to contact my company manager?"

"I've got a bone to pick with you, Levi." John said, before his boss could go any further.

"I hope it's a cosher bone."

John grinned despite himself. He remembered that those of them who knew Levi well had a collection of what they called 'Levi's levities' which they would exchange from time to time. Levity had been in short supply a few days ago when he'd been told he was to have an assistant. He thought that this conversation might not be too light and humorous either.

"It's a cosher complaint, Levi. What am I supposed to do with this girl, Moira? She knows nothing, seems not to want to learn, gets in the way half the time..."

"John, John, I told you. I want to make her take some of the strain from you."

"Frankly she's just creating more. Come on, level with me, what's the real reason? You and I have been in this business long enough to know she's not part of it. What are you playing at?"

There was a surprisingly long pause. The line hissed slightly, and faintly you could hear dialing pulses in the background. John heard what might have been a sigh at the other end before Levi said, "I can't tell you at the moment. Do me a big big favour and run with it for the time being. I promise I'll fill you in as soon as I can. Take care." and he hung up.

Hung up without discussing whatever it was he'd rung to say, without any of the usual discussions about box office returns and local press reviews, arrangements for the stars to appear on local media, venue contra charges and artists occasional temperamental grumbles.

John put the receiver back in the rest very slowly and gently. Then he sat and stared into space, puzzling over what might be going on. He noticed the cooling coffee, tried it, discovered it was a bit lukewarm now, found a hip-flask, and enlivened the drink from 'white with three' to 'white with three and a generous helping of scotch', knocked it back in one, and went out to take the cup back to wardrobe.

He spent the rest of the day blissfully free of Moira. He lounged in the stalls for the technical run through, making a few notes, but there seemed to be no serious problems despite the complexity of the show which they ran as a cue-to-cue, missing all those chunks of the show where no seriously important things involving the cast were due to happen. Gathered around the production desk in the middle of the stalls, he, the touring lighting designer, the sound engineer and the musical director all agreed the change to The Royal had gone very well. He could see Moira in the semi darkness at the rear of the auditorium near the sound desks apparently examining the contents of a flight case that was still parked in the main aisle. He dismissed it. 'As long as she's away from me', was his thought.

The afternoon brought the dress rehearsal. It was a bit mechanical and lifeless. The cast had arrived piecemeal about lunchtime. Most had found their dressing rooms, and then wandered onto the stage to look out at the highly decorated auditorium, A few, who had not played The Royal before, expressed delight at the opulent décor. The players with the more demanding vocal parts were prone to stand on stage and make a variety of noises, 'to try out the acoustics'. The leading lady sang a few lines of 'Come back love' experimentally. It amused him, as they had no cause to complain since the theatre dated from the era when the architects somehow 'got it right'. In any case 'Chuzzlewit' was carrying extensive sound equipment, so the way the building behaved for a solo voice was almost irrelevant to the performers. John slightly regretted this. He accepted sound systems for the electric rock musicals, but often felt that shows with conventional orchestras and casts that could sing perfectly well if left to their own devices probably didn't benefit from a mass of technology. Theatre was in a change-over, from the days when sound meant subtly reinforcing a few weaker aspects to achieve a good balance, to the newly accepted style of having everything amplified and the audience well aware that it was.

They ran the show right through. The cast obediently said their lines, sang the songs, danced the dances and moved where the blocking dictated, but the could see that they were only marking it. First night in a new city would bring it all back to life he was sure.

The curtain fell on the last bow, and almost immediately flew out again at stage management's request. John shouted from the stalls "Thank you very much ladies and gentlemen." and the choreographer ran on stage to pre-empt the rush to dressing rooms to make some minor point about one of the routines. Stage management, he knew, would be chasing the resident crew up about a couple of scene change details, but he trusted them to deal with these.

"All happy?" he questioned the gathering around the production desk, receiving nods as the desk itself was being dismantled to clear the stalls seating ready for an audience. John looked at his watch. Only just over an hour to curtain up. He remembered he hadn't eaten yet today, slipped through the pass door and went to the office to pick up his coat.

Moira was standing outside, reading the label on the adjacent door. She'd been very quick leaving sound and getting backstage he thought.

"Hello Moira. Did you learn anything from the run, then?" he asked.

"What's 'Mollie's Garden'?" she countered, without any opening pleasantries.

"Had a good day with sound?" he repeated his question.

She shrugged. Seeing that she still had no small talk he answered her, "It's the kids' show that's playing under us here for a couple of weeks."

"Under us."

"We do the evenings, they do some matinees."

"So there's going to be another show here at the same time as us? That's inconvenient."

John was unsure what would be inconvenient for her, except sharing an office, and as she hadn't been asking for an office he didn't think she meant that. He said, "Yes, sorry, you'll have to share the 'Assistant' office with their company manager for a whie I'm afraid. But Mark's a nice bloke, and he'll only be here in the daytimes when we don't have a matinee but they do, so you'll probably not even overlap."

"I'd intended to use the daytimes... No, never mind. It doesn't matter. Have you met him before?"

"Oh yes, this has happened a few times on the tour."

She gave him one of her hard searching looks.

"Anyway, now we are properly in I'd like you to be with the house manager. Get all the returns and so on, and see if the advance is OK and if not what he's done about extra publicity."

John knew there was hardly a seat to be had for the duration of the run at The Royal, but he thought it would be good for her to see what went on front of house, and good for him to keep her out of the way.

"And find out when press reviewers are in and, if you can meet them, try to butter them up."

She was hardly someone he would have put forward for a public relations job, but he also knew that any provincial reviews would hardly affect already full houses, and only locals read local press, so it could do no damage to later dates on the tour. Her look was sour, almost suspicious. Maybe he was being unkind. Gritting his teeth he said, "Look, it's gone the hour, do you want to come for a quick bite to eat?"

She shook her head, and any such plan was immedately disrupted anyway by one of the cast, one of the older ladies in the chorus, coming along the passage saying, "Oh John. Can you help me find some digs?"

He said 'sorry' to Moira and led the cast member into the office, saying, "Have you tried the stage door list?", knowing full well that she would have. She said, "Yes, but I need something twin bedded, because my daughter's had to come to stop with me this week for the half term break and she comes some weekends too."

John nodded understandingly. One of those single parent families with a working actress mother and a child in boarding school he supposed. Now he thought about it he had occasionally seen this cast member, Irene she was called.. the name came to him.. accompanying a girl at café tables, or front of house tea shops, even in a backstage corridor once, despite the usually strictly enforced rules about visitors. He remembered the daughter as a sullen looking young teenager. Well, maybe she did find digs, and the general boredom of strange cities to drag round during daytimes, tedious. He found his 'digs' file, rummaged to the appropriate city, and ran his finger down the close typed lists. The pages had started off as the standard issue digs list from The Royal, but biroed additions, notes and alterations had turned it into a much more detailed and extensive directory. He turned the last page over, to where added addresses and contact numbers mainly showed. Selecting one he picked up the office phone, dialled nine for an outside line, and when the external dial tone came he rang the number he had his finger under. A few moments of enquiry, during which he had to ask how old the woman's daughter was, and he could report success to Irene. He hung up, gave her a note of the address and told her that the landlady was waiting for her, and would be happy to keep an eye on the daughter during the evenings, (babysit was too young a word for a thirteen-year old he thought), and warned his actress that, although it was only two streets away she would need to hurry to be back in time for the half.

Irene was full of grateful thanks, and dashed away to check in. He saw that Moira still loitered just outside his door, having clearly been observing the little scene.

"And that," he told her, "is just one example of the infinte and exciting variety of our company management lives." He was being flippant, but was also sure that she didn't really understand this. Abandoning humour he said,

"You might want to have a wash and brush up before the half."

"Are you saying I look mucky!"

"I'm saying it's a first night, and I assume you're going to come front of house with me, partly to meet the house manger, and partly to sneak in the back and watch the show."

"I've seen the show..." she stopped seeing his look.

"And, all things being equal, you'll see it again and again."

She muttered 'OK' and went into the assistant's office. He washed and changed into a black suit, not quite evening dress, but with a bow tie, and combed his hair. On any other first night he would have showered and shaved but somehow that long standing, comforting, routine had been disrupted for him by Moira's presence and attitude.

He chided himself for breaking his own traditions as he rubbed his chin, feeling the slight stubble. He couldn't recall the last performance that he had not approached with his simple ablutions and change of clothes. There was something reassuring about having deliberately taken the time to prepare, to be ready, for the special event about to happen. Now, ominously, he felt he missed that feeling.

He need have had no concerns. As he had anticipated the cast rose from their mechanical rendition of the earlier dress rehearsal to the performance level he expected. Technically all the aspects of the show gelled perfectly, and the audience reaction was, as they had all become accustomed to, nothing short of rapturous, culminating in the, now familiar, standing ovation. The local house manager, even when introduced to Moira, had smiled and welcomed her to 'his team' as if he were genuinely pleased to meet her. His professional bonhomie did little to alter the woman's dour outlook on the proceedings, so far as John could see, but at least she didn't argue with the way she had been shunted over to front of house. At the obligatory first night supporters' club buffet after the performance she somehow managed to be conspicuous by standing still, not mingling, and surveying the room full of eager theatre-goers quite suspiciously.

John went over to her, asking "Everything all right?".

She rebuffed him sharply, "Why shouldn't it be!"

"Well, first night parties.. you know, a bit of a duty call for us. And you didn't look as if you were enjoying it."

"I'll survive," she snapped, "but I'm not likely to find anything out here."

He thought 'find out' was a strange expression, but left it and returned to mingling. He failed to notice the number of cast members who were either actively avoiding, or giving dicouraging looks to Moira. Somehow the feeling had already spread that she was a cold fish, and some people were detecting quickly that she was also apparently a fish out of water.

Theatres all operate a very tight backstage security system, and the Royal was no exception. But the arrival of each new touring show creates a confusion until the passes are issued and the stage-door keeper has become used to the cast and crew faces. Some of the company hardly needed passes, their famous faces being a good enough means of gaining acccess. Some, like John, were so familiar to stage-door keepers that they would mostly be waved through with a cheery smile. The comings and goings of a get-in weekend, emcompassing a swathe of short stay casual workers, truck drivers and hangers on, always test the arrangements to limit access to the general public. Because of the slight confusion that arises on a Sunday when a show changeover is taking place the odd individual slips in. So it was that, having come in through the stage door with Lucy Gainsborough, the wardrobe assistant, during the get-in, Eddie Gainsborough, her father, was recognised, and nodded in, late in the first week of 'Chuzzlewit's residency.

He would have waited at the stage door for her to be paged, but it turned out to be unneccessary. Eddie strode confidently toward where he remembered Lucy having shown him the wardrobe was. It was John who happened to meet him in the orange passageway on stage level,

John knew he'd seen the man before somewhere, but a fleeting encounter in the pub mid-way through get-in had not registered too well. He vaguely remembered he had seen the stranger as part of the crowd with Lucy on Sunday lunchtime. Had she said he was a family member?

"Hello," John said, and from habit when strangers did occasionally turn up backstage, added, "Do you know where you are going?"

"Hello John," Eddie replied. "I've just been taking a parcel to Lucy."

The man spoke with a London accent. John had assumed that the family came from here because Lucy had said they lived in this city. Was this her father he puzzled? He remembered being introduced now. Obviously the other man had paid more attention as he knew John's name.

He muttered something non-commital, thinking the man would make for the stage door to leave, but Eddie said,

"Look, you must come to ours, well Bill's, for Sunday lunch this weekend. Everyone would love you to come and we always have a big family get together every weekend."

John hesitated. He was tempted by the thought of a Sunday meal that wasn't a pub lunch, but he really hardly knew these people. He remembered his resolve to get to know the cast and crew better but..

"Do come. Lucy would be so pleased."

"That's very nice of you but I couldn't impose on..." He stopped, as Lucy appeared from the doorway to wardrobe further along the passage, "Ah, Lucy. I'm being persuaded to come to Sunday lunch."

"Has Daddy asked you, oh good, I told him he should. You will come won't you."

Lucy arrived beside them with almost childish eagerness, and John found himself agreeing.

In the other direction along the passageway he saw Moira. She was standing very still watching them. Like a predator silently stalking its prey he thought. He couldn't quite discipher her expression. Anger? Concern? It was certainly not casual, nor was it friendly. Who did she have such dislike of? And how could she have built up such an obvious feeling in the brief time she had been with 'Chuzzlewit'? Was it jealousy of Lucy? He liked Lucy. In a fond, distant, fantasising sort of way, he recognised that he fancied her, but they'd hardly exchanged more than a few words till now, though the fleeting exchanges they had shared had been friendly enough, perhaps he could convince himself they were almost flirting. No, it couldn't be that.

As he puzzled over this Eddie, after being assured that John would come to Sunday lunch, turned to leave and John saw Moira abruptly back away around the corner of the corridor to vanish from view. He had no doubt that she was ducking out of sight, but why should she not want John to see her? Or was it Lucy, or Eddie she was avoiding? No, it couldn't be Eddie, he was not part of the company, and John couldn't imagine anyone in the company having any dealings with an outsider, especially in the few hours that had elapsed since they rolled into town.

Lucy was telling him the address, and instructing him to come at midday so there would be time for a drink before the meal, and he scribbled the address on a scrap of paper he found in his pocket. Eddie's back retreated towards the stage door. He turned briefly at the corner to the lifts and waved, and moments later they heard the metal slither of the lift door opening. Lucy went back to the wardrobe, and John stood there quite near to his own room, contemplating the little scene that had just played out.

Half an hour later Moira came into the office. She didn't knock. She entered and closed the door purposefully behind her leaning against it as if to keep him captive.

"How do you know that man?" she demanded, without any preamble.

John decided to wait before telling her to mind her own business.

"Which man?" he asked disingenuously.

"You know exactly which man. The one you were talking to outside here."

"Oh him. Just an aquaintance."

"Where do you know him from? How long have you known him?"

These seemed very searching questions. He looked at her quizzically. "Why? What's wrong?"

"I have to know what you have got to do with him."

John felt like going on the defensive, but decided to play along with what seemed like an interrogation.

"Not a lot. Just met him really. What's this all about?"

She hesitated as if she didn't want to explain, then said, "You should stay away from him, that's all."

John was taken aback at this statement. "Should I now?" he said pointedly, "And who exactly says so?"

"I can't tell you any more, but take my advice and steer very clear of him."

"Where do you know him from then? Come to that what do you know about him?"

She seemed stumped by questions, maybe because it reversed their roles, and said, "Just be warned." before slamming out of the office.

John was totally puzzled by the incident and what Moira had said. He took out the whisky bottle and poured a generous measure into a used coffee cup.

Chapter 4

He walked to the theatre from his hotel the next morning, after a leisurely and substantial breakfast in the rather smart hotel dining room.

As he approached the building he saw a van pull away, apparently from the curb near the stage door. It bore the wording 'Dog Unit' on the sides. John only caught a glimpse, but it roused his curiosity briefly. It didn't sound like the sort of business vehicle he expected to see at a stage door.

Making his way inside he greeted the stage-door keeper and said, "What's that all about? Got a rat problem?"

The man shrugged and looked distinctly grumpy, saying, "Not any more, the rats have just left."

John looked at the old man quizzically. Funny how stage-door keepers are usually old men, he thought.

The man shuffled in his little glass fronted office and as if wanting to change the subject, said, "Doesn't matter," adding, "There's some post here for you, John," and pulling a thick bundle of different sized envelopes from one of the pigeon holes beside him. John sifted rapidly through the envelopes, and said, "If these are the best you've got you can keep them."

"You haven't won the pools then?"

"Looks like the box office returns that weren't ready at the last venue," he waved an envelope, "some advertising," he raised another, ""and I bet at least these three are begging letters from wannabe actors or actresses who'd like to be in the show. Anyway I'd better go and deal with them, but I won't shoot the messenger. Thanks."

And giving the dog unit van no more thought he made his way

briskly up the stairs towards his office clutching the post and gently rubbing his wrist with his free hand.

Later in the week Nicole and Laurence knocked on the door of that office, and getting no reply opened it and peered in. They had used all of Laurence's celebrity to get this far into the theatre, and were willing to wait it out until John should re-appear from wherever he had gone off to. The stage door keeper had tried to locate him by phoning different places in the building, but without success. It was only really the pressure of other calls and visitors, and Laurence's celebrity status, that had won a grudging 'Go on then.' from him which had allowed them in. Finding John's office for the season had been easy, now they hesitated on the doorstep.

"Come on," said Laurence, "we'll wait for him inside." and without looking to Nicole for agreement he went in and sat down on one of the room's utilitarian chairs. Nicole followed and paused as the door swung shut behind her, taking in the rather bleak décor, and hard furnishings and the business-like desk against one wall, piled now with the paperwork that a major show generates. The rooms in this theatre were not warm and welcoming she decided. As usual the company manager's office had been created from a dressing room, in this case quite a large one, with the addition of a desk. It showed its alternative function by the work surface shelf around most of the walls, and the naked light bulb surrounded mirrors above this. Nicole found a reflection of herself wherever she looked.

Laurence told her to sit down, but she wandered about the room looking at this and that until her eye fell on a dog-eared copy of 'Spotlight' on the desk. She picked it up carefully.

"Perhaps they're looking for some new cast members." Laurence suggested. "Hey, there's a thought. John could put in a good word for you."

She looked at him with those slightly plaintive eyes which he had once found appealing, but which now regularly irritated him. He was sorry, for her sake, that the show they were in was coming to an end. But he had his next play lined up and he'd be leaving for London directly the curtain fell on the last night of the run here. She could stay on in the flat they'd rented of course, or she could come with him into London digs. Either way he was toying with how to tell her to pay her own way. It had been a good enough affair, and he'd managed to wangle her work on the shows he'd appeared in. Her appearance in the current one as the maid amounted to little more than a couple of lines but satisfied her by keeping her in work and near to him, for her attraction for him had not waned quite much as his for her. Nicole still fancied him a bit, but she was not infatuated as before.

'Perhaps it always wears off.' she thought to herself, as she idly turned 'Spotlight' over in her hands. As she did so she noticed a page was bookmarked with a slip of paper. Curiosity led her to open the volume.

The double page was divided into eight, four sections to a page; the lower budget adverts. Each section showed a black and white picture of the head and shoulders of a hopeful artist, with their name in bold type, a paragraph with details of the more notable venues played, and the address of their agent and contact number.

One of the actresses on the marked page was Penelope Carson. The photographer had caught exactly that slight aloof tilt of her head that had so annoyed and fascinated those who had known her. Her blonde hair was longer in this photo than it had been when Nicole and Laurence had worked with her in the small touring show that John had been company manager of, hanging just below her shoulders, which were bare. The picture was cropped just above where any top she might have been wearing would have started so that there was a mildy titillating effect, of possible nudity, intended to attract the attention of casting directors.

Nicole had a realisation that the book was not on the desk by casual accident, and that its presence with the marked page showed that she had been right. John had not overcome the loss of Penelope which had heralded the abrupt end of that Theatre Wagon tour of 'Eyre' on which they had all met. She held the book out towards Laurence, open at the dead actress' entry.

"Look. There's a bookmark at this page."

As she did so the door opened and John came in. For the briefest second he paused, taking in the presence of his two former company members, and the book Nicole was holding. Then very quietly he took the book from Nicole's hand, closed it and laid it carefully back on the desk.

Softly he said: "Hello you two."

Laurence was all bluster. He made great noise and bonhomie about how good it was to see John again, explaining that they were at the theatre on the opposite side of the road until the next weekend, managing to supply the information that he was off to London immediately their current show closed, and making no mention of Nicole. Nicole felt embarrased. She was embarrassed by Laurence's loud insensitivity to discovering John's continuing grief. She was embarrassed by having been caught with the copy of 'Spotlight'. She was embarrased by the old feelings that rose inside her at seeing her former lover, no boyfriend; what was the right description?

"Hello John." she said meekly.

They stood, facing each other, hesitant, a foot or two apart as Laurence ploughed on, suggesting that they should all go for a meal together.

Ignoring Laurence she suddenly blurted out, "Oh John!" and wrapped her arms around him, burying her face in his jacket and starting to sob. She felt him putting his arms round her so they were hugging each other. Then she was conscious of the whiff of whisky on his breath as they kissed. Laurence, still seated fell silent.

After a few moments he said, "We were very sorry about Penny."

"Penelope." John corrected, in exactly the tone of voice that Penelope had adopted so often when people had used the shortened form of her name.

"Whatever." said Laurence off-handedly. His manner ignored the abrupt way the tour they had all been on had ended, and the fact that they had not seen John at the time. Ignored the fact that he and Nicole had not seen John since the accident, failing even to attend Penelope's funeral because they had so rapidly got parts in a play. "Anyway Nicole wanted to come and see how you were." He didn't claim that he had wanted to visit.

John disentangled himself from Nicole, who looked pointedly at Laurence because of his insensitivity.

"That's kind." John muttered, making his way round the side of the desk to the chair behind it. The movement failed to entirely hide his wiping the back of his hand across his eyes. "How have you been getting on?"

"Well 'All Invited To A Murder' isn't exactly a great play, but we've done good business round the circuit..."

"Laurence's name on the billing has helped a lot." Nicole interjected loyally, despite frowning at the direction Laurence was taking the conversation.

".. and as I said we close on Saturday. I'm going straight up to town to start on my next show, it's another murder-mystery, I'm afraid, and there doesn't happen to be a part for Nicole in that. You're not looking for an actress I suppose?" he laughed to imply that he was being flippant, though, clearly, he was really deadly serious.

John shook his head slowly, staring down at 'Spotlight' on the desk in front of him. There was a long pause.

"How's 'Chuzzlewit' going?" asked Nicole, in an attempt to keep up some sort of conversation.

"It's fine. I know it rather well, of course. For some reason they've given me an assistant." He shrugged. "I can't think why."

Nicole wondered if the promoters were worried about John's state of mind. Now she had seen him she knew she was. She also remembered what he had told her about why he knew 'Chuzzlewit' so well. Maybe he shouldn't have agreed to revisit that show she thought. She went round to his side of the desk and squatted beside his chair, putting an arm around his shoulders. He turned his head towards her, and she caught the whisky smell again. Now she looked into his face she could see his eyes were slightly red ringed and there were new lines, that made him look older than he had done.

"If Nicole stops here in our flat, rather than coming to town with me, you two could go out for the odd meal together while you are here." Laurence said. "I wouldn't want her to be lonely."

Nicole leant her head against John's cheek. He could feel her hair next to him. She'd dyed it a little darker and it was closer to brunette now than the natural mousy colour it had been. There was a noise at the door.

"I expect that'll be my assistant now." said John, as the door opened.

It wasn't. It was Lucy. She paused, framed in the open door, taking in the scene: Laurence lounging, so far as was possible in a hard chair, John behind his desk, and Nicole clinging closely to him.

"Oh, sorry," she said, "I'll come back later." and she made a hurried exit. She paused in the passage outside. She had recognised Laurence, of course. His pictures, larger than life, adorned the frontage opposite and were hard to miss. Who was the girl, so attached to John, she wondered. Were they together? She hoped not. There had been no rumours of him presently being in any sort of relationship What she had seen of Laurence, cooly ignoring the embrace, made her wonder about the relationships between the trio. It worried her more than she wanted to admit.

In the office Nicole studied John's reaction. She tried to interpret his expression. Her inate insecurity made her wonder if this was a new girlfriend.

'Why should I mind?' she asked herself, 'I'm with Laurence, John's not mine any more. Perhaps it would be good for him to have a new girl.' but in the back of her mind she knew that her being with Laurence had soured, and that this visit to John had already emphasised the cracks in the space of a few moments. Seeing her former love had brought all her old feelings back... except.. When they'd been together it had been John looking after her. Now she thought it was he who needed caring for. She wanted to be the one doing the caring. She remembered the dozens of tiny considerations he had shown her, even when she had told him that she was leaving him for Laurence. Why had she done that? Now she realised it had been more hero worship and lust than love, and with part of her mind she regretted it. Clearly Laurence had no qualms now about going off to London without her. Some of his references to the coming separation implied he would welcome the break, and he hadn't tried very hard to persuade her to come with him, insisting mostly that she should stay in their flat, almost like a caretaker.

There were perfectly good reasons for her to remain, and keep the flat ready for Laurence's weekend returns, she accepted. Well, at least, if he did return at weekends, she thought. Perhaps he would prefer to remain in London. Perhaps he would find a new girlfriend in London. Perhaps... It seemed to the young actress that Laurence no longer wanted her around. There, in that room, with John present, she finally accepted that from Laurence's point of view their relationship was effectively over, and she now regretted splitting with John. She realised now that his good nature had been much more valuable to her hesitant and nervous disposition. Laurence had driven, even bullied her along her career path, while John had always been sensitive to her needs. Now a worrying period of 'resting' loomed in front of her.

Laurence said, as if the interruption hadn't happened, "What do you think?"

John, who had been distracted by the door opening, looked back down at the top of Nicole's head, resting now on his chest and said dully, "Yes we must, that would be nice."

The conversation lapsed. After a pause Laurence said, "Well, we must be going." at which point another brusque knock, and immediate opening of the door revealed Moira. Without waiting for introductions she said, "Who are these?" to John. It was abrupt, forthright, actually rude.

"Nicole and Laurence were in a little touring company I was managing some time ago," John explained.

"I'm sure you know Laurence Drover," Nicole, who had raised her head from John's chest and was trying to look as though there had been no intimate contact a second earlier, gushed, "he's a TV star."

Moira looked at Laurence, and back to Nicole.

"I see." It was a quite suspicious sounding phrase the way she delivered it.

John said, "Can you go to the house manager and check the programme sales with him."

"Where is he?"

"In his office I expect."

Moira gave him one of those sour looks and left.

"Se doesn't seem to very friendly." Laurence remarked as the door shut. Maybe Moira heard, maybe she didn't.

John shrugged. "I'm not sure why I've been given her as an assistant, as I said. She really doesn't help."

"Oh poor John!" Nicole sympathised, "Perhaps she'll get better."

"Perhaps there's some nepotism going on" said Laurence.

"Perhaps," said John, "but I can't for the life of me work out who is high enough up the organisation to swing her into an invented post."

They all paused, John and Nicole both considering this, although Laurence had lost interest. Another bang at the door, another interruption, this time a minor query about tomorrow's orchestra calls, and it became evident that Laurence and Nicole were in the way. They both stood to leave, Laurence saying, "Here's the flat phone number, just give Nicole a ring during your show's run. She'd love to have a catch up with you. You're here for six weeks aren't you?" he turned to her, without waiting for a reply, "You'd like that, wouldn't you?"

She nodded obediently, and studying John sadly she said, "Yes. Please ring me." and kissed him quickly on the cheek before they both left in a disorganised flurry of 'goodbyes'.

John turned his attention back to his work and the show, gently sliding 'Spotlight' to one side on the desk.

Chapter 5

Lucy's brother's home was an unexceptional semi-detatched house in an area that had once been quite smart and expensive, but had somehow slipped into drab and worn. As he walked up the street John could see that there were properties that had clearly been owned by the same people for decades. He guessed that these were mostly retired couples on pensions. In many cases paintwork was cracked, and some of the prim net curtains on the front bay windows were yellowish with age. Scattered among these were a few really startlingly badly maintained ones, with untidy dustbin strewn front gardens, broken gates, even the occasional smashed window, and there were some where the owners were clearly making the best effort they could. Lucy's brother's was one of these. The front lawn had been mown, although it was strewn with a few bright coloured childrens' toys, and as he went up the path to the door her realised from the freshly turned earth that someone had recently been planting things in the borders.

He had brought two bottles with him, in view of what he had gathered from the wardrobe staff about the possible business struggles of the launderette, and these clinked together as he freed one hand to ring the doorbell. He heard a sudden murmer of voices inside when the bell rang, which he guessed amounted to 'Can you answer that?' because the door opened almost immediately to reveal a boy of about ten in a football shirt and jeans, who looked back over his shoulder and shouted to someone invisible "It's a man with some bottles."

A woman appeared through the door at the end of the longish hallway, which was decorated with slightly old fashioned flowered wall-paper. She was wearing an apron and carrying a saucepan, and the smell of roast dinner followed her out of the kitchen into the hall.

"Hello, you must be John. Do come in. I'm Alison, Bill's wife."

John said 'Thank you' and came in, wiping his feet and shutting the door behind him. The football fan had vanished into the room on the left, presumably the living room. John offered the bottles,

"I brought a small contribution." he said.

Alison's 'you didn't need to do that' was mainly drowned out by what seemed to be a crowd bursting out of the kitchen and living room. There was the launderette owner, who John now vaguely remembered from the previous weekend in the pub during the get-in and now guessed to be Bill. The man who he knew to be Lucy's father, and presumably Bill's as well, but who's name had still failed to register in his mind, came out with a small girl clinging to his leg shouting 'granddad', and Lucy herself, smiling in welcome and thanking him for coming and helping Alison who had become encumbered by taking the bottles while still holding a saucepan.

The family swept him into the living room, a long through-lounge with a laid dinner table at the far end, parked him in a chair belonging to the three piece suite, also floral, like the hall wallpaper, and, behaving as if he were some important visiting dignitary, supplied him with a drink within seconds.

John, who spent his life organising small crowds of performers into entertaining large crowds of audience was quite overpowered by the family. He found himself unable to put up any resistance to the insistant hospitality. He surrendered to the onslaught. The boy who had opened the door, who turned out to be, confusingly, called Bill, after his father, started an excited explanation about what yesterday's football results meant for several teams that were nothing more than names to John, as soon as he was seated in the deep soft armchair. This was interrupted and shouted over by others in the family trying to ask John about the show, about his food preferences, and about where he came from and what his family background was. If he had not been on the receiving end of an in depth lesson on English football he would have felt under interrogation.

Lucy's father, Eddie turned out to be his name, eventually cut through the onslaught with a 'Cor, let 'im drink his drink you lot.' John had the feeling that the London twang had been exaggerated for some reason. He noticed that Bill had a similar but less strident accent.

"Were you brought up in London then?" he asked him.

"I came up here a long time ago, just after Alison and I got married. She wanted to be near her Dad you see, but he died soon after, and we never moved back."

"You did right, lad. It's not the same any more, There's too many villains about nowadays," his father put in. "Not a place to bring your kids up in."

Bill expanded on this sweeping statement, "We've got a cousin in the same line of business as me in London. His launderette has had the windows broken five times in the last six months. One night they drove a stolen van right through the front of the shop."

John thought he just heard the father mutter, 'He should have paid.'

Alison said, "I would worry too much about the kids if we had to move back there now," and, adding, "Must just go and look at the dinner," she vanished toward the kitchen.

"Anyway," Bill said, "you can't just go and open a laundrette wherever you like, you'd soon find yourself in competition with someone... on their patch, so to speak, and it's taken a long while to get established here."

"Well, we'll try to put some work your way while we're in town. What made you go into that business?"

"Oh the family has always done some laundering," Bill's father said, and gave John a wink, which made John unsure how literally or seriously to take the comment. He decided it must have been flippant. In either case he was now being pressed about his background in theatre and found himself talking about his favourite subject, musical shows.

The time passed and the drink flowed until Alison started urging them all to the table. He found himself seated between Lucy and the little girl, who announced that she was Emily before starting to talk excitedly about theatre and shows she wanted to see or had seen, for it seemed her parents took her to the theatre quite often. Auntie Lucy being in town with a show meant that Emily expected to be taken to see that too. John doubted the little girl would understand 'Chuzzlewit', he hardly followed the convoluted twists himself, he thought wryly, but he made a mental note to sort some comp tickets for the family.

Alison and Bill were on the opposite side of the table with young Bill at one end, and Eddie at the other end, which they clearly considered to be the head. It was a generous meal, and conversation, even from Emily, lapsed somewhat as it was eaten. John found himself luxuriating in the unaccustomed situation: a good Sunday roast meal, not concocted by himself in some microwave or produced by a commercial kitchen, and social chatter with people who, he had to concede, he was coming to like more and more.

Between courses, while Lucy and Alison cleared plates and brought out exceptionally generous portions of jam sponge and custard, Emily resumed her chatter, telling him how she was going to be a set designer when she grew up, because she liked drawing and painting, and how she was practicing at the moment with her toy theatre. He asked her about her toy theatre, and she wanted to show him, but Alison said, "Finish your dinner first."

"What sort of shows do you want to do?" he asked.

"Musicals. Musicals about princesses," the child replied.

"Quite right," he said, through jam sponge, "people want to see nice things like that."

Bill, who'd been following his daughter's explanations, said, to John, "So why are serious plays and opera so successful then?"

John felt himself warming to his favourite soap-box, and tried to stop himself, because he didn't think that the family really wanted him to put forward his views on the good and bad aspects of the world of theatre, but still found himself saying, "The snobs think that serious plays are 'worthy' and that opera, for example, should be encouraged because someone has decided that it is 'good', so those sorts of things get big grants thrown at them to make sure they keep getting done. The public, the great unwashed, don't want worthy stuff, so they pay to see light frothy happy things, like Emily says she wants to do."

"What's a snob?"

"And you always work on popular shows then?" Bill asked,

"Sadly, no..."

"What's a snob?" Emily asked again insistantly.

"Someone who thinks they are better than you," Alison told her daughter, with the air of someone who spent much of her time having to offer explanations to an inquisitive child.

"Bill's a snob then, 'cos he thinks he's better than me," she announced loudly, "snob, snob, snob."

"I'm not, and you don't know what you're talking about..." her brother protested, but his grandfather held up his hand in an unmistakeable 'stop' gesture and said, "Just leave it, Bill."

"Popular shows?" his father reminded John.

"Not always, no. We can't always afford to choose. But I'd rather not do shows with a message, or those that are being done because some director or company has a policy that they think is good for the public, so that rules out the classics and nearly all acclaimed modern playwrights."

"Chuzzlewit?" somebody asked rather critically.

"True," he said, "but we've built up the 'happy ever after' ending in this production, and there's some nice tunes."

"Coffee everyone?" Alison asked.

There were murmurs of assent all round.

"What's wrong with modern playwrights?" Bill wanted to know.

His father muttered, 'Good question, what the hell _is_ wrong with the modern playwrights?'

John said, "What's wrong with them is they all want to make a political statement. Personally if I were to go to the theatre as a member of an audience I'd want to be taken out of my everyday life and shown something happy and amusing. Sell me a couple of hours of joy, not a couple of hours of lecturing. Anyway, enough of this, that was a fabulous meal," he looked at Alison, who was collecting dishes. "Thank you so much."

"You're welcome," she said, "Lucy did it as well."

He looked to the wardrobe girl next to him and saw that she was studying him much more intently than such an informal get together might have implied. Was her family match-making? Had he been ignoring her throughout lunch by getting involved in other conversations? He gave her a warm smile and said, "Thank you," and her face lit up briefly.

After the coffees the children were restless. By some unspoken mutual agreement the party broke up. Alison and Lucy made off into the kitchen and sounds of washing up could be heard. Bill, his father and son went outside with a football 'for a kick about'.

Emily was eager to show John her 'theatre'. She went to the cupboard under the stairs and dragged out a cardboard box, which she positioned on the floor away from where her mother was still coming and going clearing the table, saying 'come and look!'

"I hope you don't mind," Alison said to him as she passed.

He shook his head and got down on his hands and knees on the floor with the girl.

It was a very simplistic 'theatre' at first sight, just an old cardboard box with a rectangular hole cut out of one side to form a crude proscenium arch. When he looked closer he realised that someone had helped in its construction. Someone who knew something about theatres. Emily had drawn rather wonky pillars on the cardboard either side of the 'proscenium' and added a shield with trailing ribbons above. If you looked into the box you discovered that she had painted a number of backcloths on drawing paper. Someone had sellotaped a couple of drinking straws across the top edge of each of these paintings, sticking out at either side so they could rest on the edges of the box and the 'backcloth' would hang in a position on the stage. The wet paint had caused the paper to crinkle and curl, so it was all rather untidy but the concept was there.

He encouraged the girl to tell him about it. She launched into the plot of some fairy tale, changing the 'backcloths' as she did so. Suddenly she stopped and said, "I've got to get the actors," and dashed out. He heard her stamping quickly up the stairs, then coming down again, more slowly, because now she was carrying arms full of cuddly toys.

"This is the princess." It was, inevitably, a doll with a sparkly dress. She placed it centre stage, where it failed to stand up so she laid it down, "She's having a rest," Emily excused it, "and this is the baddie," she produced a sad looking teddy, "he's not really bad, he's just acting being bad," she explained.

She lowered the bear through the top of the box so it appeared next to the doll, "But he has to come on from this side," she said, "stage left," she announced, proudly.

"Quite right," John told her, "clever girl. Who told you that?"

"Auntie Lucy said so. And she said they sometimes call it..." she fumbled for the word, "prompt side."

"Did Auntie Lucy tell you what they call the other side?"

"Opposite prompt, of course," said the child in a tone that implied 'didn't you know that?'. Then, "Do you love Auntie Lucy?"

John was aback at this. He hesitated, wondering what he should say.

"She loves you," Emily announced.

Jonh saw Lucy appear in the doorway. It was clear she had heard this statement, she was blushing very red. He tried not to catch her eye as he told Emily, "Well that's nice." and, trying to bring the subject back to the theatre again asked, "What do they do in your show?"

Emily said, "They sing." and without warning launched into song, letting go of the teddy so it fell on its back, and standing the doll up and holding it so it seemed to stand centre stage.

She started to sing 'Come back love', the hugely popular, rather hauntingly catchy solo number from 'Chuzzlewit' that had been in the music charts for many weeks during the original production. She sang childishly, and slightly out of tune, but clearly knew every word of the somewhat complex lyric, though she parrotted the unfamiliar words without understanding in places. She sang through the whole of the first verse, and then a chorus.

As she got about half way through the verse, and seeing that she was going to go on, John pulled a little maglite torch from his pocket, turned it on, and pointed it at the doll, adjusting the beamspread so it seemed to be a followspot. Without pausing Emily leant forward to see the effect. It was quite dim in the room so the torch showed up brilliantly on the toy stage. When she came to the end of the chorus he tightened the torch beam to a very narrow spot and snapped it off, as would often be done at the end of a musical number for a solo singer.

Behind him Lucy clapped, and Emily dropped the doll and crawled to him saying, "How did you do that?"

He showed her the torch, and how moving the front collar made the beam wider or narrower. She played with it, saying "That's neat!" before looking up at Lucy. "Can I have one of these for my theatre?"

"You can have that one," said John. Seeing Lucy start to protest he said to her, "I can get another."

Chapter 6

When the footballers came back inside John felt it was time for him to leave, heaved himself off his knees and to his feet, and with more 'thank-you's and protestations that he must come again he made for the door. Lucy said she would walk with him as she felt like some air, and they left together.

They walked in silence till they were well away from the house, then both started to speak at once. He let her go first.

"Emily didn't know what she was saying back there," Lucy told him.

He laughed softly. "It was very flattering," he said, looking across and down at her, for she was a head shorter than him. Her shoulder length hair blew across her face as she looked up to him.

"I wasn't sure what to say to Emily when she asked that question though," he told her.

"Emily's world is full of princes and princesses and fairy godmothers and everyone falls in love and lives happily ever after," Lucy said.

"Perhaps everyone's world should be like that," he said, thinking sadly of his own life.

They had reached the kerb ready to cross toward his hotel. She grabbed his hand. "We do know. About, you know, things that have happened. Lots of us really care."

"That's not love. That's pity." he told her, rather brusquely.

She looked stung, but bravely persisted. "I didn't get to talk to you at lunch, Emily's such a chatterbox. Can't we just go and have a drink somewhere?"

The street had that Sunday shuttered and closed look. Over the road his hotel at least had some lights on in the foyer. Still holding hands they crossed the empty road and went in. Reception was deserted. He had a quick look in the restaurant in the hope that they might be serving afternoon tea, but laid-up and deserted tables told him that this was not the case. He led her to the lift and they went up to his room.

John always stayed in hotels rather than bed and breakfast digs when on tour, partly for the convenience of access to telephones and being able to leave paperwork laying about, and partly for the extra comfort and service usually available.

Lucy, more used to cramped rooms converted from standard bedrooms into two, to allow the landlord to cram in more paying guests, in bed and breakfast theatrical accomodation, looked enviously around. John made straight for the table with the tea making things on, filled and boiled the kettle, and dunked tea-bags.

"White with?"

"Yes please." She sat on one end of the settee.

He peeled the tops from the tiny milk cartons and once done put the cup on the small table beside her. He brought his own tea to the settee and sat beside her. She had wondered if he would take the armchair to avoid being close.

"I think I could put up with touring if I could afford digs like this." There was an undercurrent of jealousy in what she said.

"I need some of this for the job," he told her, "anyway I'm too old to slum it."

"You aren't really old," she told him

"Compared to you I am."

"You've done loads more than I have, but you aren't old. Are all the rumours true," she asked bravely.

"I don't know what the 'Chuzzlewit' rumour mill says," he said.

"That you've done 'Chuzzlewit' before and someone hurt you, and that you were on another show where someone got killed..." she gabbled quickly to get the unspoken questions in before he stopped her. "I'm sorry I shouldn't have asked," she had seen the look in his eyes.

The sun was setting outside. He stood up and went to the window, shutting the curtains, turned a desk-light on so the room felt warmer, opened a cupboard and brought out a bottle of whisky, waved it at her and when she shook her head poured a generous slug into his tea. Then, back beside her on the sofa, he told her all about the first production of 'Chuzzlewit', slowly at first and then opening up in a sort of catharsis brought on by her sympathatic silence and the lunchtime wine, of his marriage and divorce, and then of Theatre Wagon, and eventually of the accident that had killed Penelope.

"Is that what the rumours all say?" he asked when he had finished. A lump had formed in his throat again through talking about Penelope.

"Something like that."

"Well now you know, and you see why you shouldn't be trying to take on a lame duck like me. Even Levi seems to be trying to give me a easy ride, even if it isn't working.. he chose the wrong person with Moira," He checked himself, "No, forget I said that. What I think of Moira is none of your business."

"Levi Fischer?" She ignored the 'none of your business' and he had another pang of guilt at having used too strong a phrase.

"Yes." The way she had said the name betrayed her awe at the man's reputation. It showed him how different were their worlds, he rubbing shoulders with the entrepreneur producer, she scraping a living, and he knew exactly what she earned, washing and ironing. Cinderella flashed through his mind. But he was no prince.

"Listen," she turned more toward him and took the hand that wasn't holding his drink in both of hers, "Emily said 'love'. Well I don't know what you think, but I believe that love is caring about the other person and wanting to help them. And that's how I think about you. You can brush it aside and say I'm too young to understand, but I care, I really do care!"

He thought she sounded like some sort of agony aunt, but the lump in his throat was still there and threatening to become embarassing.

"If nothing else let me be an ear, or a shoulder."

"Lucy, you are very sweet..."

"Don't!" she said. "No buts.. just if you want," a pause, "anything." and she placed a single finger on his lips to stop him from answering back.

They sat like that for a long moment, before she took her hand away again and unexpectedly pulled out a handkerchief and burst into floods of tears. He had no choice but to put the cup down and take her in his arms.

When she stopped crying she said "I'm sorry." and then, out of the blue, "Who was the girl in your office when Laurence Drover was there when I came in?"

So she'd noticed Nicole then, thought John. And remembering Nicole he felt another surge of sad emotion. She was, he assumed, on her own this weekend after Laurence had left for London. He had an imagined vision of her sitting sadly and forlornly in

Laurence's flat. He wondered if she had been waiting for him to ring her, because he was almost certain that Laurence wouldn't. 'What a collection of lame ducks we all are.' he thought. What really upset him, he supposed, was that despite repressing the feeling of awful loss that Penelope's death had produced for months now, it had only taken the sight of Nicole and some well intentioned sympathy from a wardrobe assistant to reduce him to his low ebb again over the course of a weekend. Moira was just a nuisance, no worse in her way than some of the hundreds of irritations that he had encountered at venues and with members of casts over the years. He knew the solution to this upset. As always he would have a few drinks and then sleep it off.

"Laurence Drover?" Lucy reminded him, calling him back from these thoughts.

"Yes, Laurence. Well he was in the little touring adaptation of Jane Eyre. And Nicole was in the cast too."

"Just in the cast?"

He hugged her a little tighter. Softly he admitted, "No, not 'just' in the cast."

"I didn't think so when I saw her with you."

"When companies are touring it's not unusual for people to pair up," he said, "In big companies, like this one, it usually only affects the couple in question. In small companies, and 'Eyre' was very small, friendships and fights affect everyone."

"Was she a 'friendship' or a 'fight'?"

"Do we have to do this? I mean... Look, I said that what you felt for me was pity. So perhaps that's what I felt for Nicole. It's not a recipe for a solid relationship."

"She left you?" Lucy asked perceptively.

He nodded. "But there was Penelope.." He was annoyed with himself for the weak way his voice came out saying this.

"But you still fancy Nicole don't you."

He thought how can she read so much into a fleeting moment seen through a dressing room door? Anyway he wasn't sure about Nicole.

"You can't go back," he told her, "If you did it wouldn't be the same."

No, it wouldn't be the same, because there would still be no Penelope, he told himself.

"Don't try to go back then," she said, "Move on, have some fun, try to forget."

But that was half the problem, he didn't want to forget, he wanted to remember. To remember every minute of those few brief days, and save them forever. He understood now that the whole day had been staged so as to try to get him to agree to 'fun' with Lucy, whether out of sympathy for his situation or for her benefit he couldn't be sure. He looked down at her head nestled against him. He had no wish to hurt, or even disappoint her but...

He freed an arm, picked up his cup and drank. The tea had gone cold, he drank it down because of the whisky in it.

"Do you want some more tea?" he asked, "This has gone cold."

She said 'no', and went on, "I thought you fancied me a bit."

Yes, he did, he thought. He said, "Are you staying here, or going home tonight?" It was blunt, but it put the decision back in her hands.

"I think I better go back to my digs, Another time perhaps we won't have raked up so much history." She was very grown up and decisive about it.

The level of the whisky bottle went down after Lucy had left.

Chapter 7

The lorry with 'Mollie's Garden' in it was in the street by the loading doors one morning later in the week when John arrived at the Royal. 'Chuzzlewit' had continued its run, doing great box office business and receiving the usual standing ovations. Backstage John and Lucy had smiled distantly at each other as they passed. John thought Lucy's expression might have been wistful, Lucy thought his might be regretful. They hadn't spoken since Sunday afternoon. Brenda and Alice, in the steamy heat of the washing machines, watched Lucy carefully, trying to work out what had gone on. They analysed the situation into possibly they did, and now he, or maybe she, regretted it, or possibly they didn't, and now he, or maybe she, wished they had. Brenda and Alice puzzled over the situation.

Moira, now instructed to sit with the lighting operator for a few performances to watch the show from there, was achieving a bad reputation for nosiness. John had thought her off-hand manner from the start had been disinterestedness, but he'd had several crew members bend his ear, saying that they kept finding her poking into cases in the scenedock, and sometimes, in the case of LX and sound, beside the control desks. Challenged as to what she was doing opening boxes she had reverted to her curt defence that she'd been ordered to find out about things. What things still seemed a grey area. The technicians were understandably annoyed by her behaviour, especially as it seemed that her nosy curiosity frequently led to her shuffling the flight case contents. Repeatedly John found himself apologising and saying "I'll have a word with her."

John met Mark in the stage door. They swapped pleasantries.

"'Mollie' going all right?" John asked.

"Yeah, no problems, apart from those bloody sponge heads. They're a begger to wash, 'cos they take an age to dry, and they get all sweaty inside, which plays havoc with the radio mics."

John nodded sympathetically. "I've had to put you in with my assistant I'm afraid, but she's hardly ever in the office so..."

"Assistant? Since when did you get an assistant?"

"Since Levi insisted. Don't ask me why. Anyway the door stickers are there for your usual three rooms."

"Thanks. I'll catch up later, must get this lot unloaded." and the kids' show company manager hurried away.

Moira appeared from the street. He had to give her credit, she did seem to turn up a lot at times when there was no performance and she might have reasonably stayed in her digs.

"Your co-habitee has arrived with the kids show. He's called Mark. I've told him you two are sharing."

Yet again she failed to acknowledge what he was saying and muttered something about looking at the understage. She called it the cellar, but he realised what she meant. He wondered why, but made toward his office. On a whim he went past it and along to wardrobe.

"Hello Brenda," he said, looking about and finding that neither Alice nor Lucy were there.

"John," she said, dumping the costume she was carrying onto the sewing table, "coffee?"

He said 'please' and the woman went to the kettle, fussing with mugs and coffee jars, saying over her shoulder, "You're not messing young Lucy around are you?"

"Why, what has she said?"

"It's more what she hasn't said. I know you were going to her brother's for Sunday lunch, but she clammed right up when we asked about it, and she's not been herself the past day or two."

"I'm sorry, it's probably my fault."

"I thought it might be. What have you done!" Brenda demanded firmly.

"Oh I don't know. We had a nice meal and then she walked back to town with me and... Well I guess she came on to me."

"Of course she did. She fancies you like mad. I'm telling you that because we've known each other a long time."

"Well...I didn't do anything..." He found himself on the defensive.

"You rejected her, you rat. It took all that courage for her to show she was interested in you and you 'didn't do anything', just turned her down. Here's your coffee."

"It wasn't like that. It was, complicated."

"About your past?"

He nodded.

"John, you've got to snap out of this. I don't care what's going on in that head of yours... No dammit I do care, we all care, but if you start brushing people aside you start upsetting them as well. By the end of the tour we'll have a company where they all want to crawl into a hole and get drunk, not just you."

"I don't think there's very many of the cast who fancy me, and I don't get drunk, I just have a few drinks," he protested.

Brenda snorted, "Much you know. Haven't you seen the way the chorus look at you... yes and the male dancers too!"

"Oh come on!"

"Sorry but it's true. From the company's point of view the best thing that could possibly happen would be for you to pair up with someone. It doesn't even have to be one of the cast. An outsider from the city even, but at least everyone would know where they stood. Oh I know that things didn't turn out too well when we were both on the first 'Chuzzlewit' and you got hitched to that," she fumbled for a word, "woman," she said, with venom, "but put it behind you. People like you, really they do."

"I didn't know anyone was interested enough in me to bother..."

"Everyone is. Everyone always has been, on every show. Especially now after what happened. And you don't notice. You're too bound up in hiding in your work. It makes you the best. And it makes you unbearable."

"Brenda, why haven't you said something before? We've known each other for years, you should have been able to."

"Because you haven't upset one of my staff before. Please get Lucy out of this moping, we need her, you need her, probably, especially after the... accident, even if you think you don't. Now take that coffee back to your office and leave me to mend this jacket in peace."

He left, in a very subdued and thoughtful mood.

Frank came in after a while and they checked through the show logs to make sure there hadn't been any recurring glitches, but the resident crew of The Royal were keeping everything running very smoothly.

"No problems fitting 'Mollie' in?" John checked.

"No. I've been with them all morning and everything fits OK. Well we knew we'd left the right spaces anyway. God! Who'd drag round with a thing like that, lumpy great costumes, squeezing your set into the space left by a main show, making do with wherever the house LX rig happens to be pointing, and playing tripe to screaming toddlers."

"You're selling it very well," John joked, "By the way I'll see if I can help Mark out on his costume problems by pointing him at Lucy's brother."

"Our Lucy?"

"Yes, her brother runs a laundry. They're doing our bulky stuff while we're here. Didn't you know?"

"I find it best not to get involved with wardrobe unless I have to. Bound to tread on some toe or another if you poke your oar in there. Brenda scares the life out of me."

John grinned. "I know what you mean."

Moira burst in through the office door without any preamble and burst out with "There's a couple of our flight cases down in that cellar that are locked."

John and Frank looked at each other and back to the woman.

"So?"

"Well what's in them"

John said quietly "I'd guess they were either LX or sound spares. If they're sound they might be the stock of radio mic batteries."

"Why are they locked?"

"To keep prying eyes and sticky fingers out probably," Frank told her sharply. He stood up to leave.

"I'll have an ask around, and find out" said John.

Frank looked at him puzzled. "Well wouldn't you think it sensible to lock up small nickable things?"

"Yes, Frank. I would."

Frank shrugged and left. John said to Moira, "What's the big deal?"

She said, "I think in my position I need to know what we are transporting about the place," and she too left. A moment later he heard the next-door office door slam.

He dug out a bottle and poured himself a drink. Even he thought it was still a bit early, but he felt that it had been that sort of morning. The show relay system was active now and he could hear Mark and his cast and crew sound-checking. He guessed that they had already run through 'Mollie's' simple scene changes with the resident crew. The show only had a couple of lighting states so Mark would have no problem plotting them before a late afternoon matinee.

He saw Lucy passing towards wardrobe and ran to the door, calling after her, "Lucy."

The girl turned, he thought, reluctantly.

"Can I have a word?"

He saw her look at her watch before coming back to his office door.

"I'm really sorry about Sunday," he started.

"So am I," she said, "I shouldn't have..."

"Yes you should, and I'm a fool. Can we.. well you know."

She nodded in a rather brusque way and began to turn away.

"You know 'Mollie's Garden'."

"If you want us to go and watch it together you can forget it," she told him. It was almost a joke.

"Perhaps we could do better than that," and not giving her a chance to answer he went on, "would Bill be able to do some more costume cleaning. It sounds as though 'Mollie's' company manager, you know Mark don't you?" she shook her head, "anyway he needs the foam heads cleaned between performances. Shall I give him Bill's number, or would you like to?"

"If I get Bill to bring our costumes he's got today to us, instead of me fetching them they could show him what they want," the girl suggested.

"Clever girl. What time will our cossies be ready? I'll go and tell Mark."

"Any time now I should think. I'll go and ring him."

"Ring him from here," John said, "Nine for an outside line."

Leaving her to make the call he went on stage. He felt a bit out of place walking into the other show's set even if they were only sound checking. Brightly coloured, flat painted, over-sized flowers and foliage dominated the scenery. He poked his head cautiously around a wing looking for Mark, who saw him, waved and came across stage toward him. An actress wearing one of the sponge heads with a huge smiling face and over-large eyes, surrounded by a cascade of sculpted sponge curls, was centre stage, her jeans and tee shirt sticking out below the head incongruously. She spun to face John, still reciting some piece of script for the benefit of sound, and studied him through the gauze panel in the smiling mouth that allowed the operator to see. John found it unnerving.

He said to Mark, "Sorry to butt in. Your head washing.... Do you want our local laundry bloke to come and have a word with you to see if he can help?”

“Yes please!” and he raised his voice to instruct, “Just run a bit of a number.”

“I'll sort it out then,” John promised, as a loud tinkly tune started up in the foldback and the actress's amplified voice began singing.

“He'll be with us in about half an hour,” Lucy said when he got to wardrobe and told her.

Brenda and Alice watched this fleeting exchange like hawks. John felt he was under surveillance and left.

Chapter 8

Moira said, "Did you find out what's been hidden in those cases?" when John got back to the office after sorting out the cleaning arrangements for Mark and the 'Mollie' company. Bill and Mark had both been grateful. John hoped, in a way, that Lucy was too.

It was late in the afternoon. The schools were out. An excited audience of children could be heard from the show relay system speaker. Mark and his company had got the show in, set up, and were now about to give their first performance here in The Royal. On future days they would give two, or sometimes even three, performances in a day, except when 'Chuzzlewit' was running a matinee, but today was probably the most frantic and exhausting for them and their company manager.

John studied Moira. 'She's very obsessed about those cases', he thought. "No, I haven't got round to that yet." He thought perhaps he shouldn't stifle any enthusiasm she might have, weird though he thought it, so he said, "Come on, show me which ones you mean."

They went down the stairs instead of the lift, past the stage door level and into the understage. The stage floor above their heads reverberated irregularly from the cast's footsteps as 'Mollie's Garden' performed above them. Once in a while you could hear the excited shouting of the children in the audience.

"Over here," said Moira.

There was a fair sized pile of cases and storage boxes of all shapes and sizes. He saw that two had been pulled out from the rest and now stood slightly separate. Each had one of its catches locked by a cheap combination lock. John laughed. "I bet..." he said.

He bent and twiddled the combination dials of a lock, squinting slightly in the gloomy understage to see the numbers. There was a click and the lock opened. He took it off and opened the lid. A pile of boxes of batteries half filled the interior. "See, batteries for the radio mics," he told Moira.

She grunted unhappily and asked in her sharp way, "How did you know the number?"

John laughed. "Sound department, one-two, one-two. Just a lucky guess. Happy now?"

"What about the other one?"

He shrugged, shut and locked the first case, then opened the next using the same number. It was nearly empty, with a few boxes of small spare parts at the bottom. Moira reached in and took out a coloured box with pictures of microphone clips printed on. She opened it. It was full of microphone clips.

"You're very nosy, or very suspicious. Which is it?"

"I have to know what's going on don't I?" she snapped at him.

"Look, I'm pleased if you are keen to learn, just try not to get side tracked into these little details." He was interrupted and drowned out as the bass beat of one of the childrens' show numbers thumped through the woodwork above them and the cast began dancing about, adding their footsteps to the din.

Moira shrugged and muttered something that might have been "Just doing my job," before turning away and leaving John on his own. Sighing he shut and locked the second case and wheeled both of them back against the pile.

The thumping on the stage floor above him stopped and he could hear the applause. A moment later a single thud downstage announced the house tabs reaching the floor for the interval. Feet pounded about overhead and he heard the unmistakable sound of truck castors travelling across the stage as the crew re-set ready for the second half. John left the stage basement and started back up to the less dusty parts of the theatre. He nodded to the stage door keeper as he passed street level and made his way back to the company office.

When he got there the door to the next door room he had assigned to Moira and Mark was wide open, and he could see the woman sitting at the dressing room shelf writing industriously in a small black notebook. He thought she must have seen him reflected in the mirror in front of her, but she ignored him.

He too busied himself with some paperwork, and it did not seem long before the end of show applause could be heard over the dressing room speaker. The 'Mollie' cast were audible, clattering about on the stairs leading to the next floor up where their rooms were, and after a pause, Mark returned to his room carrying a case. John got up and followed the kids' show company manager into his room.

"Everything go all right?"

"Thanks, yes, great show. Lovely audience."

"I know, I could hear them."

Mark laid the case on the table and opened it, beginning the process of removing the batteries from the radio mics that were inside. ""Oh, and thank you for sorting the cleaning of the heads. Lucy's arranging for them to be picked up now. She's good, isn't she? She suggested some places for extra ventillation and she's agreed to do some modifications for us over the next few days."

"Don't steal her when Brenda wants her, I'll never hear the last of it. And don't forget to pay her," John said, wanting to be sure that Lucy's helpfulness wasn't being taken advantage of.

"I won't. I mean look at this mic!" he held up a flimsy headset that was clearly damp. "Even if it doesn't help the mics survive the cast will welcome a bit of a draught inside the stupid things."

Moira was listening to the conversation. She leant across to peer into the microphone case. John thought 'she really is incurably nosy'.

"Who else has access to this case?" she suddenly demanded of Mark.

Mark looked bewildered. "Why?"

"I just wondered," said Moira.

John could see Mark puzzling over the woman's question. He could see the moment when Mark decided he'd better say something. He said, "I guess anyone in the 'Mollie' company really, but I usually dole the mics out to them at the half. It's good to make sure they're turned on. Leave it to an actor and you can guarantee they'll eventually flick the switch the wrong way or fail to think of turning it on at all."

John said, "How very true that is. We've even had our people turn the things off after they've been issued, and when you ask them why they say they thought they were helping."

"Anyway you're lucky, you've got a sound engineer. I have to share that job with my ASM."

"Is that still Justine? I haven't seen her around yet."

"Nah!" Mark threw a handful of used batteries noisily into the bin, "She left us in Newcastle. You don't want some used batteries do you?... No I guess you've got enough of your own."

John ignored the battery offer, "Shame, she seemed a nice girl. Was it something you said?" he joked.

"If I'd known you were interested I could have tried to persuade her to stay. Anyway maybe Elaine is what you'd call a nice girl. Actually we got this new ASM and new radio mics at the same time. The damp had all but written the old mics off.. though we're still carting them around. You don't want to buy them as spares do you? All nicely cased up. It was Elaine's first job when she joined... to pack them away."

John had seen Elaine backstage. She wore dungarees and had a cropped hairstyle that made John think she was trying to be male. Not his type at all.

Moira said abruptly, "I'm going for tea," and marched out, without inviting anyone to join her.

Mark said something that sounded like 'unlike some' under his breath, and carried on removing batteries.

Moira strode firmly toward the stage door. Near the lift she encountered Elaine, laden with sponge heads from the 'Mollie's Garden' costumes. There was a brief impasse as the corridor was too narrow and neither was sure which way the other was heading. While the women were still blocking the passageway Bill stepped out of the lift. He had some 'Chuzzlewit' costumes over his arm in big plastic bags. The traffic jam became more awkward. Bill and Elaine exchanged 'sorry' and Bill said, "Are those the heads from the kids show that I've got to get washed?"

"Oh, are you Bill, the laundry man?"

Moira paid more attention, studying him blatantly and carefully.

"Yes," he indicated the armful of garments he was carrying, "I just need to drop these off in wardrobe, then I can take your stuff away."

Elaine turned to Moira. "You're something to do with 'Chuzzlewit' aren't you? Could you take those down there," she nodded along the passage, "then Bill and I can manhandle these damn things down to the stage door... I guess you're parked out there?" she asked Bill.

Moira hesitated, and then held out an arm for the costumes. Bill loaded her with the bulky dresses and said 'Thank you."

Elaine and Bill divided the sponge heads between them and by the time the lift re-appeared at their level Moira had vanished toward wardrobe.

"She doesn't seem too friendly," commented Elaine as the doors rattled shut.

"No. I've heard about her, though I hadn't seen her before, Lucy says she's some sort of assistant company manager. Not a very popular member of the company from what I have heard."

"Who's Lucy?"

"My sister. She's on the wardrobe for 'Chuzzlewit'."

"Ah. That's how you got the cleaning work."

Bill nodded. "Very likely, you can't beat a bit of nepotism," he said. The lift juddered to a stop and they took Mollie and her friends' heads out to his car.

Just after the half that evening John rounded up Moira and explained that he was going on a tour of all the dressing rooms, and he thought she should accompany him so as to meet all the cast. He had thought she might be reluctant to trapse around the building, but she surprised him by laying aside her earlier sulleness and following him almost meekly.

They started in their own corridor, which aside from wardrobe and the company offices held the star dressing rooms, both at the end nearest the lift and stairs and with the most immediate access to the stage itself.

John knocked on the first door they came to. Anthea, the show's leading lady shouted 'Come in' and he opened the door. Anthea had settled into the star room very thoroughly, filling available shelves in the sitting room area with personal bits and pieces, framed pictures, a few greetings cards and all the paraphanalia of stage make-up. She turned now and, seeing John, rose and said, in that slightly artificial way that some members of the acting profession seem to adopt, "John, darling, what a nice surprise!"

"I just dropped in to make sure you'd settled in all right... and to introduce you to Moira. Moira, Anthea, Anthea is our leading lady, Moira, just joined us as my assistant."

Anthea looked Moira up and down with a superior air and said, "Assistant? Since when did John Mason need assistance?"

"Oh I don't know. Levi seemed to think I needed some help."

"Levi Fischer? Well you can bet your life there's something in it for him then. No offence dear," she addressed Moira, "but he hasn't arranged this for either the benefit of the show, or to help John. And you don't need help," she told her company manager, "eveyone knows Levi's got himself the best with you."

"That's very kind, Anthea, But it seems Levi's got other ideas. Anyway I just thought you ought to know who Moira is... can't have you thinking there is a stranger wandering about."

"Oh, it might liven things up if there were. Relieve the boredom, you know," John felt he there was a suggestiveness behind the suggestion of 'relieving the boredom' given the way Anthea looked at him as she said it, but she was right, repeated performances could get monotonous. Maybe the show was at that point now.

A faint murmur from the show relay speaker indicated the first members of the audience starting to come in.

"Can't stop, we want to try to get round everybody before we go up." her told her, and they left amid goodbyes and break-a-legs.

The scene was almost exactly repeated at the next room where the leading man, Oscar, also expressed disbelief in John requiring any help, although without calling him 'darling'.

As Moira left the dressing room, where again she had not contributed to the chat, Oscar put a hand on John's arm and whispered in his ear, "Let me know if you want to get rid of her, I'll just tell Levi she's a waste of money." and he winked.

They walked up the stairs to the next floor. The yellow level housed the rooms of the more minor characters. There were a mass of them, and the time ebbed away as he repeated his enquiries after the cast members' welfare and introduced Moira again and again. He began to notice that not only did Moira never offer any conversation to the cast, they failed to take more than a minimal interest in her, responding with the barest formality to the introduction. 'What is it', he wondered 'that puts people's backs up on first sight like this?'

Up another floor where the ensemble members of the cast were divided among several large rooms he made introductions there too, although he didn't tell Moira every name, though he probaby knew them all. They found the rooms in this green corridor in a concentrated state of preparation. Not any sense of panic, but the determined professionalism of people who knew exactly what needed to be done before an immovable deadline. Still every room broke off briefly to greet John, and give a wary 'hello' to Moira. One or two of the chorus girls flirted with him, and a couple of the male dancers made suggestive remarks, though they did so in the certain knowledge that they were wasting their time.

"Ladies and gentlemen, this is your five minute call. Five minutes please," the measured voice of Tania the ASM came down the tannoy system.

"I'll leave you all to it," John told them, "have a good show." As they left he said to Moira, "We'll meet the orchestra tomorrow."

"I've looked round the pit, there's a lot of cases there I need to keep an eye on."

John studied her suspiciously. "What's this fixation with cases?"

She stumbled over an un-convincing explanation. "Well I might need to know what's going on the trucks when we move to another town." She saw his questioning look and said, "You wanted me to keep a count on the orchestra stuff before."

It was true, he recalled, though it had only been an attempt to give her something to do.

Performances came and went. John found that the show's number 'Come back love' was squirrelling around in his head. Sometimes it caused him to smile fondly, remembering Emily, innocently singing it at Lucy's brother's house. Sometimes the song's lyric dredged up unwanted memories of relationships or affairs that were now, for whatever reasons, over.

He tried his best to encourage Lucy. They were both working full time on the show and there was little chance for social chit-chat. He wished he hadn't given her the impression that he had turned her down completely. The location of wardrobe with its access past his office meant that he saw her hurrying back and forth frequently, but not to speak to. On one occasion he grabbed her arm as she passed,

"Stop and have a tea break," he said to her, "come to the foyer café with me."

The girl hesitated and then gave a slight toss of her head, which reminded him painfully of Penelope, and said, "Another time perhaps. I've got to fetch the ironing."

It wasn't, he convinced himself eventually, the outright rejection he had feared.

Later her saw her struggling with another of the huge boxes of soap powder by the stairs down to the stage door. Moira appeared through the door from her room.

"That's another box of detergent," she said to John, "they can't be using that much."

"Might be to do with 'Mollie's Garden' as well," he said.

"No. There's something suspicious about that."

He thought she was making a joke for once, but when he looked at her he saw that she was deadly serious. By the time he looked back along the corridor Lucy had gone.

"And then there's her father," Moira added.

"You don't like him either do you?"

"I don't like gangsters. No forget I said that," and she strode off along the corridor before he could ask what she meant.

Chapter 9

In the latter part of that week at The Royal John was in the company office. It was late morning, and they had no matinee, he was in the theatre through force of habit, and because he had nothing to amuse himself with in the hotel. He really didn't need to be on site till tea-time. 'Mollie's Garden' would be playing in the afternoon.

He was clipping the show's review from a copy of the local paper to slide it into a clear plastic wallet ready to store in the ring binder full of such press cuttings. As ever the local reviewer had been fullsome in his praise for the show. Words like 'triumphant' and 'stunning' were liberally scattered down the column. Naturally Anthea and Oscar each received special mention, but he was pleased for the more minor players to see that the press hack had made great use of his copy of the programme to name many more of the cast. A bit of encouragement never came amiss and he could guess that copies of the paper would be circulating backstage that night. He was closing the file when he got a call from the stage door. The unexpected ring made him jump.

The door keeper at that moment was a middle aged woman, the daytime staff. "There's a woman here to see you," she told him. The night-time stage door keeper, seasoned professional that he was, would probably have told him who was visiting.

"I'll come down," he said, and set off. Somehow he guessed it would be Nicole before he got down the stairs.

She was waiting by the door-keeper's hutch in the lobby.

She was wearing a plain, straight, camel coloured coat, much better than the one he remembered her having had when they were with the TIE show, over what was very obviously a dress that she had given a great deal of thought to. The dress was smart, but not a business suit. It was brown, with cream trim, but not a party frock. It fitted in all the places that mattered, but it wasn't tarty. Nicole had made a great effort. He had a mental image of her spending much time in front of a mirror trying to strike the right note. He had to admit that she had been very successful.

Her first words were less assured, "Hello John, I hope you don't mind me coming like this, I mean.. is it inconvenient?"

He smiled. That was the Nicole he knew. Uncertain and nervous.

He said, "Do you think it's too early to go for lunch?"

She looked at her watch, giggled, and said, "Perhaps, it depends how far we've got to go to find lunch."

He took her to his hotel. It was only a short walk, and they were the first diners in the restaurant, but the tables were laid with the shiny glasswear and cutlery and thick cloth napkins that he remembered had impressed Nicole on the pair of occasions that they had eaten in places other than 'greasy spoon' cafés in the past.

It was a bit strange, he thought, how the scale of the show they had been together on, and therefore their respective wages, had limited the occasions on which he and Nicole had dined in anything other than a café. He decided her nervousness at any sort of remotely elaborate table setting had probably been overcome by now. He didn't think Laurence had been eating in tea-bars over the past months. Maybe she had been cooking for them in their flat? But he remembered her rather basic abilities with cooking too, remembered how to her opening a tin and heating the contents had been a small triumph, and remembered how he had thought of those failings as endearing. Laurence wouldn't have thought that, he was sure.

He stood by the table for a moment while the waiter seated Nicole, and then sat too. They were asked about drinks. He looked at the girl, who said, "Just water, thank you."

"Are you sure," he asked, "No particular reason is there?"

He remembered the misunderstanding on that night when she had been trying to tell him she was leaving him for Laurence, when he had thought she was trying to tell him she was pregnant. Now, again, he wondered if this was the case.

"No, no real reason," she said.

He changed the order to glasses of wine, and she didn't protest, slipping back into passive acceptance of him arranging her life for her; of him caring for her.

They had walked to the hotel with hardly a word spoken. Now, once they had ordered, they sat silently, each waiting for the other to start. After a few moments they both spoke at once,

"John..."
"Nicole..."

They stopped, and laughed, and the reservations were broken.

"You first," he said.

"I didn't know if you wanted to meet up. I mean Laurence was so pushy about it when we saw you, and I thought, perhaps, you didn't want to see me..."

"Of course I wanted to see you," he was only half lying. If he were honest his mind had dwelt more on Lucy over the past days, and he had some concern now that Nicole might be a complication. He had already explained that she was just an 'ex', could he convince Lucy that she was no challenge to any faltering relationship that might, or might not, be on the horizon between him and the wardrobe girl? He felt uncomfortable, particularly as he was now very aware, sitting opposite Nicole, how much he was still attracted to her. If Penelope were still here... But no. He had to stop thinking like that. And there was Laurence. He couldn't place Laurence in the confused mess this threatened to become. Was Laurence's off-hand behaviour toward Nicole just how he was, or had he truly tired of her. John remembered warning Laurence to look after the girl, but he had no idea how their relationship had been since then.

"I should have got in touch," he apologised, "but, well you know how it is with shows."

She nodded. Yes, she thought. He's still the same, the show comes first, but there's something more. Now the show is a shield and he's hiding behind it. She'd never thought of John being anything other than outgoing and confident, but some spark had gone. Gone, she assumed, with Penelope's death. She saw him rub his arm, and the action raised his cuff enough for her to see the scar that started on the back of his hand and ran under the new watch and up his arm.

"I don't want to push in. I mean in all this time I expect you've made new friends. New company, new friends."

"Not really," he told her, "Some of the cast and crew I knew already. The new people, well they're all OK. But no new friends. Not in the way I think you mean anyway."

"The girl who came into the office the other day when Laurence and I were there, what about her?"

"Lucy? She's from wardrobe."

"And?"

"And I don't know. I probably put her off a bit. I know Brenda thinks so."

Nicole didn't ask who Brenda was, but said, "She's very pretty."

"Mmm," he said non-commitally, and "Thank you," to the waiter as their meals arrived.

He had noticed that Nicole had ordered quite confidently from the over flowery menu, swiftly choosing the roast rump of lamb with goats cheese ravioli, without waiting to see what he would pick. He assumed that she had eaten out a great deal in her time with Laurence and had become more adept at working out what was meant by the French languge spattered hyperbole.

"Laurence won't come back, you know."

He stopped with his fork half way to stabbing the first piece of 'confit of pork', which actually just meant pork chop. He saw that there was hurt in her expression.

"Of course he will," he tried to reassure her.

She shook her head. "He was bored of me, and he didn't want me to go to London with him. I've had a lot of time to think about it and I'm sure. Anyway I think it was a foolish infatuation on my part."

John nearly said 'I think so too' but restrained himself.

"He'll be back. You've just hit that awkward patch when one of you is working on a new show."

"If 'Eyre' had carried on I think we'd have gone our separate ways at the end," she looked at John to see if it was alright to mention the end of the little tour but he was hiding any emotion by eating, "As it was Laurence lined up work for us both, together, very quickly."

John swigged some wine and rubbed his left wrist for a moment before returning to the food.

"I was so infatuated with him I'd have followed him anywhere," she hestitated, "I do still love him, I think, maybe, but it's not the same."

"Nothing stays the same," John told her quietly.

"Do you remember when we went to your friend Isaac's antique shop looking for props?"

"Did he tell you it was an antique shop?" John asked with a slight return to his original fire, "it's a junk shop, and he knows it."

"As we were leaving he made me promise to look after you. And I haven't and.... Oh John I'm so sorry!" she dropped her knife and fork onto her plate with a clatter that caused a few turned heads from the scattering of other customers who'd arrived while they'd been sat there. The self control she had been gripping so firmly since she came to the stage door asking for him suddenly collapsed into self pity.

John laid his cutlery down more carefully, drained his glass, and stood, saying, "Come on, this isn't the right place for either of us."

He led her out, collecting her coat from the lobby and assuring the staff that all was well, adding "charge it to the room" and whispering a room service request.

By the time the lift came Nicole was crying properly. A ping announced its arrival and the doors opened. They were lucky, and it was empty. He put his arms round her as it went up to his floor.

Once in his room Nicole said, "I feel such a fool, making a scene like that."

He used the room's kettle and tray of sachets to make coffee for them both, opening the mini-bar and sharing a whisky between the two cups. He brought the drinks to where she was sitting forlornly on the end of the bed sniffing.

"You've put whisky in it," she said after a sip.

"Purely medicinal," he told her. He took his jacket off and hung it on the back of the chair at the dressing table. Despite herself she grinned. The dressing table had been cleared of everything except files and paperwork relating to 'Chuzzlewit'.

"Still bringing your work home with you?"

"What else is there to do?" he asked. And she didn't know if he was joking, or if it was a sad comment on his situation.

He sat beside her, conscious that she was on the edge of letting long pent up emotion out.

"Now," he said, gently, "What would you like to happen? I mean this is a mess however you look at it, so you say what you want."

"I want it all to go back to how it was before Laurence came along."

"What? You living at Mrs Odet's and us having tea-time fry-ups in the café round the corner."

She shook 'no'.

"Later then?" he suggested, "When we were together and you really wanted to be with Laurence?"

"You're being unkind."

"I'm trying to show you it's never been simple and it doesn't have an easy happy ending, or middle come to that."

"Anyway, you'd decided you wanted to be with Penelope at that point."

Stung by the memory he said, "Yes. And that didn't last long did it." and the lump came to his throat again.

"John, I'm sorry!"

"So am I."

She wasn't sure if he was sorry about them splitting up or sorry that Penelope had died. There was a long silence.

"You see there's no point in time when everything in the garden was rosy."

Tentatively she asked, "What about Lucy?"

"I don't know."

"But you know what you want?"

"I like her."

"You fancy her." The faint hope of getting back together with John was fading.

"Oh all right, yes dammit. And that's another complication. I, sort of, led her to think we might... and then I stopped it. And now everyone thinks I'm a right, cad."

He used the old fashioned word after a brief deliberation. There was a tap at the door. He jumped up and collected the bottle that room service was delivering.

Nicole watched him sadly as he got glasses and poured generous measures of whisky. She shook her head, "No thanks. You shouldn't either John," but he pressed the glass into a hand only just that moment freed of the coffee cup. As he held the glass out to her his sleeve slipped up showing the scar. She took the glass, and held his wrist with her other hand.

"Is this from, you know, the accident?"

He nodded. She ran her finger along the scar. "Oh John!" she said again, "A permanent reminder. Does it hurt?"

"The press reports and the rumours hurt more," he said. And to her dismay he knocked back his drink and turned to pour another. Sitting back beside her he said, "I guess you saw the headlines, 'Stage manager kills actress in late night joy ride crash', that sort of thing."

"Yes. We saw them. We knew it wasn't true. And the court case knew too."

"Ah, the court case. Eleven months of waiting, and then to have to re-live it all again, with the legal vampires trying to prove you were wrong, that you couldn't remember it properly. Believe me I can remember it, every second of it.." and he fell silent.

"I should have come to you when it happened, instead of going off with Laurence."

"You had your own life," he said, feeling emotion rising again at the word life. "You still have."

"You don't want me here do you?"

He didn't know. "We just proved we can't go back to how things were, or at least not to the perfect way we fondly remember it. And..."

"And you want to be with Lucy," she said sadly.

John filled his glass again and she frowned at him. "Please don't just get drunk, it won't solve anything," she begged . He shrugged and put the glass down.

"I never stopped loving you," she said, "But I was star struck."

Impusively he took her in his arms, and she flung hers around him. Within moments old passions were back. After a while he rose and shut the room's curtains.

Later he arranged a pair of house seats, and they sat and watched the show. He did this anyway occasionally to check from an audience point of view, so he called in no favours, simply used some of the company's allocation of comps.

She settled in beside him, clutching his arm in both her hands and resting her head against his shoulder as the overture played.

He remembered the last time they had sat in an auditorium together, at the Imperial. This time it was different. This was his show, and whatever the social context he was unlikely to relax his professional observation of it completely. Nicole was wrapped in the performance like a child. 'An utter suspension of disbelief' he thought to himself, and he remembered it had been that vulnerable childlike innocence that had originally attracted him to her. She had changed, he decided. The past months with Laurence had made her more grown up somehow. Now she was able to question things which affected her, while before she had been one to passively accept whatever the world threw her way. She would probably never stand up and openly defy the fates, he thought, but she'd stopped submitting without a word.

He bought her the traditional interval ice cream and they settled into the same close positions for act two. Something nagged at his mind as the show ran on. There was nothing actually wrong with the performance, but he detected a lack of sparkle. It was tricky to be precise in a show where the complex reversals of fortune for the lead characters came so frequently, but it concerned him.

'Come back love' brought the house down as ever. It was always going to, after its chart success. He concentrated on Anthea's face as she performed the number. Sometimes with a singer you felt they believed every word. Sometimes you felt they were performing mechanically, counting the bars almost. Neither of these seemed to be the case tonight. It was a competent, professional performance, but dead behind the eyes. And once he'd seen this he knew it was the case for the whole company, from Anthea and Oscar to the back row of the chorus. Someow he guessed that it was the shadow of Moira, the mysterious outsider, hanging over the company, nosing, questioning, as if they were all under suspicion of something all the time.

The show finished. The audience, and Nicole, clapped furiously, many standing to show their approval. Nicole said to him, "It was wonderful! I wanted to see the original, but I couldn't afford it because I was just a student, but it was worth the wait. Thank you." She kissed his cheek. He took her hand and led her against the flow of bodies for a few yards to a pass door and within moments they were clear of the crowd, out of the red plush and gilt opulence of the auditorium, in the orange paintwork of a stage level passage.

"I just need to go round to the office," he told her, "Wait for me at the stage door... If you are coming back to the hotel tonight that is."

"Can I?" she studied him carefully, "Just tonight, I promise, just tonight, if you'll let me."

He nodded, a feeling of guilt rising, and steered her toward the stage door, while he turned off at the lift towards the company office. There he made a few scribbled notes on a pad, turned off the light and shut and locked the door.

Lucy passed him heading toward wardrobe with an armful of costumes. She smiled at him, and he felt even more guilty smiling back.

He greeted lots of members of the cast as he went to the stage door. He felt he was lucky, though it seemed furtive, when by chance he was able to collect Nicole and slip her out of the theatre without anyone seeing her. Well apart from the stage door keeper he thought to himself. But if he knew anything about stage door keepers it was that they saw a great deal all the time and only divulged it to people they knew well, and that only when directly questioned.

They walked to his hotel again.

Chapter 10

John had been berated again by Brenda. Sometimes, lately, he was getting the feeling that he was in the wrong all the time. When this particular attack had started he had been sure that Brenda was about to accuse him of 'messing Lucy about'.

"That Moira of yours has got a nerve!"

Wearily he said, "What's she done, Brenda?"

"She only wanted to search my wardrobe!"

"Search it?"

"She came blundering in, just when we were busy," John smiled at this. It was a truism that wardrobe was a non-stop operation on the show, but it was equally understood that Brenda always said she was busy at any time of the day or night. For a second John wondered if she ever actually went back to her digs, but the woman carried on, "... blundering in, wanting to look at all the soap packets. Some fool nonsense about how much we use a week."

"I'm sorry Brenda. It's none of her business. I'll have a word with her."

'I'll have a word with Levi', he thought. 'This is getting out of hand.'

John failed to have a word with Levi. Of late the enrepreneur seemed to be more and more difficult to get hold of. John had a sneaking suspicion that Levi was avoiding his calls, which was odd, because the man was so protective of his investments that he usually wanted to know everything that was happening. John knew that it wasn't that Levi didn't trust him, quite the reverse, but the presence of Moira and the fending off of calls began to look more and more as though she had been put in place as some sort of spy in the camp. The more he considered it the more it seemed to be another possibility to fit the scenario. Which was it, he wondered, the publicly announced 'assistance' to take the strain off him, or a spy to report whether he was up to the job still, or... He felt himself becoming paranoid, and he could see why the company was seeming to feel the same. It annoyed him. 'Chuzzlewit' had been a slick and generally happy show. There had been no problems worth mentioning, and now, so swiftly after Moira's arrival, you could find irritated people everywhere. It wasn't showing too much on stage. He knew that he had only seen the fading of the performance spark because he knew the show so well. No, it hadn't shown on stage to the public, yet, he qualified that thought.

Having failed to speak to Levi he contented himself with confronting Moira, in a scene that was becoming familiar. He asked her what she meant by poking into wardrobe. She told him some unconvincing tale about it being essential for her to understand how every department worked. He warned her not to upset Brenda and her staff, and then she surprised him by saying,

"Or do you mean Lucy Gainsborough?"

Defensively he said, "Don't upset her either." He could feel pent up anger rising.

"Are you declaring an interest?" the woman demanded.

He winced at the formal turn of phrase and said, "It's really no business of yours if I am."

"It might become so. I've warned you before to keep a distance from the Gainsboroughs."

"I remember. And I remember you refused to explain, so I'm ignoring you."

"You'll regret it. You should listen to the warning. If you are lucky

I might be able to sort the timing so you aren't involved, but," she bit off her words, "No, forget I said that. Just stay away."

He didn't understand what she meant about timing, but he heard the threatening tone. Uncharacteristic anger overcame him.

"I'll see who I like, when I like. That includes Lucy. I'll give you this warning. I'm contacting Levi, and I will be doing everything I can to get you off this show. I've never had to do this before, but you've rubbed everyone up the wrong way from day one. If you have any decency at all I suggest you go to your digs for a few days. Once Levi has made a decision we'll get in touch with you."

His mouth was dry, he realised he was shouting and that, with the office door open, half the corridor was probably listening, but he didn't care. He had lost his temper, a rare event, and was furious in defence of Lucy and her family. He was surprised at himself. He hadn't realised how strongly he felt about the girl.

Moira studied him with that impassive accusatory glare she used and turned without another word and left.

From the wardrobe end of the passage came the sound of two people clapping. He knew it was Brenda and Alice. Above this he heard the sound of running feet and a breathless Lucy flung herself round the doorway from the direction of wardrobe into the office, shutting the door behind her.

"John!" she gasped.

"Sorry, did everyone hear all that?"

"Don't be sorry, please," she said and hurled herself into his arms. She hung round his neck and started kissing him. And he kissed her back.

"No-one's defended me like that before!" she told him when her mouth was free again.

"No-one should have had to defend you. I'll get rid of the woman."

"On top of everything else, you have to deal with this." she carried on hugging him, until eventually he gently disentangled himself from her and, with his hands on her shoulders, held her at arms length.

"Come for a meal after the show tonight?"

She nodded, her eyes wide and eager.

By the time the whole company was in the theatre in time for the half the rumour mill had worked overtime. That the news involved wardrobe made it spread more quickly, for every costume delivery was an opportunity for some cast member to quiz Brenda, or Alice, or an only slightly embarrassed Lucy, about the situation.

"He defended me against her," she told people. The cast gave knowing nods. In the dressing rooms the matchmakers bathed in a warm glow from the certainty they had been right.

The cast was delighted by the news of Moira's departure. Many of them had been recipients of her suspicious frowns and seemingly pointless invasive questions and everyone had been puzzled by why she was there at all. Somehow the atmosphere backstage lightened. The result was that when John stood at the back of the auditorium, watching the show, that evening he could feel an indefinable extra energy in the performance. The orchestra, who had suffered as much as anyone from the intrusive investigations of their cases and the pit itself, seemed brighter, lighter, more envigorated. The dancers had more snap. The singers sang with more enthusiasm. John nodded thoughtfully to himself in the gloom behind the back row of the stalls. Yes, there hadn't been anything specifically wrong with the show, but now, suddenly the audience were getting a better performance.

Chapter 11

John could hear anger, or was it possibly fear, in Levi Fischer's voice down the phone when he told him that he had sent Moira packing the next day.

At first Levi had told him all the same things about how she was being put on the show to help John, to take some of the strain. When John had pointed out the fallacy in that argument and listed numerous examples of her ignorance, and of ways in which her abrupt manner had upset members of the crew, of the orchestra, of the cast, his boss began to change his line. It wasn't long before Levi was admitting that he was under orders to put Moira on the show staff.

"Levi," John said seriously, "We've known each other too long for this secrecy. Who is she and who says she's got to be in the company?"

"If I tell you, my boy, you must keep it to yourself."

"I don't know I can promise that."

"Well, see what you think when you hear about it. You didn't get this from me, all right?"

"All right, it didn't come from you."

"Moira Stevenson is a police detective."

John knew the instant Levi said it that his had to be the truth, though it was a shock. He'd been prepared for some fictional explanation given how strange the whole situation had been, but this fitted the facts. He stared at a pile of programmes on the shelf round the office-dressing-room. The question remained, why? He asked.

"You ask me to break a confidence?"

"You've spilt the beans anyway now, Levi."

"The police say there's a drugs distribution network which seems to follow the path of theatre tours from one city to another. They want to find the courier to stop it."

"And they think it's someone in my company?"

"My company," Levi corrected him, "Yes that's what they tell me. This Stevenson woman was supposed to stay under cover till she had discovered who. Your little spat with her puts it all up in the air."

"I'm not taking her back!"

"I doubt it would do much good, she's too conspicuous now."

"If she had found someone what would have happened? I mean I'd have had a gap in the company if she'd arrested someone."

Levi permitted himself a small chuckle, "You always think about the show first. That's what makes you so good."

"Is there anythng more important?"

"For me and my bank account, no. For you and your welfare, maybe. How are things in wardrobe?"

"You don't miss a thing do you? Who are your spies?"

"I missed that you'd taken it into your head to sack Moira Stevenson. There's going to be big problems over that, but leave them to me. Please, as a friend, string along with anything the police request. I really don't need them poking around the show."

"Neither do I, Levi," he told his boss, and hung up, wondering if the impressario had any shady transactions tied up in 'Chuzzlewit' that would make him want to stop the police 'poking around'.

John idly moved some paperwork around the desk while he considered the phone conversation. Despite the serious tone Levi had taken over his sending Moira packing he became sure the impressario hadn't really been cross. He'd been concerned about what the police reaction would be, but he hadn't criticised John's action in the slightest. He wondered who had leaked his having taken up with Lucy. They'd been very quick to tell Levi, so it had to be someone who had the old man's ear on a regular basis. After all, he thought, there were numerous shifting relationships in any large theatre company, and one night with a girl from wardrobe was hardly of major interest to a producer. Was it?

A faint smile showed on his face as he thought of the previous evening. He'd been pleased at the renewed vigour in the cast and orchestra performances, and happy that the girl had agreed to come out for a meal. He'd been a bit afraid that his previous evident caution, and the long discussion of his past, had put her off permanently, but there had been no doubt of her eagerness to join him after the curtain fell.

As always for theatre people, the late hour when they had both finished work had limited the choice of places to eat. When they were leaving the stage door together he'd asked her about her preference. He'd hoped she wouldn't want the pretentiousness of his hotel, which might just have still been serving, though he offered it. He didn't think that the formality of that setting was quite what either of them wanted, and in any case from his point of view it was tainted by the too recent memory of the lunch with Nicole. He suggested the inevitable choice of Indian or Chinese. "Chinese please," Lucy said very decisively, and they made for the nearest one to the theatre.

There were a few empty tables, despite the post performance rush, and they were shown to seats deep inside the restaurant. Sitting facing outwards toward the door he had been able to see the arrivals while they ate, and had been wryly amused at a few members of the cast being seated. It was probably inevitable that on any random night a few members of a company as big as

'Chuzzlewit's would decide on a post show meal. It had been clear that they had noticed him and Lucy, and had done their best not to catch his eye, or show that they had seen them. He had known word would soon have found its way back into the 'Chuzzlewit' grapevine.

They had eaten, and talked of this and that. He had made Lucy talk about herself, about her family. Some he knew, some things that were divulged were new to him. He'd been unaware of the extent of her father's connections in London. He hadn't quite followed it all, but Eddie's business dealings seemed numerous and complex. Lucy herself really aspired to costume design, which was hardly a surprise to him, but she had professed herself happy with her position on 'Chuzzlewit' which was, she had pointed out, a big enough show to look good on her CV in years to come. She had chatted at length about Brenda and Alice with whom she was obviously friendly and who seemed to have protectively taken her under their wings. She prattled away happily. He sat and looked at her and listened. Nicole had said 'she's very pretty'. Nichole was right. He had a pang of concern for Nicole which was so like the way he had felt back in the days of touring with Theatre Wagon that it was almost like deja-vu, though sitting there with Lucy he felt guilt about his recent brief 'for old times' sake' fling with Nicole.

The evening established a pattern for the pair. They worked the show, then ate in some local restaurant, before going back to John's hotel. The hotel staff made no comment, even when on the second day, or night, Lucy arrived with a small case and it was clear that she was effectively moving in.

It probably didn't occur to Lucy that the hotel might want to make extra charges for there now being two customers in the room and two customers at breakfast. It occurred to John, who quietly spoke to reception and arranged to deal with an adjusted bill.

After their evening meal one night they walked back toward the hotel, but Lucy caught John's arm and led him via a side street to a small park. He wouldn't have known it was there, and presumably it was Lucy's local knowledge which enabled her to find it.

"Alice's paper said there was going to going to be a meteor shower tonight," she told him, as they made their way through a fringe of trees to a grass clearing. It was incongruous to stand in near darkness on grass, with an empty sky sprinkled with stars, above in the centre of a city. There was a muted sound of traffic on a road somewhere, and on all sides a faint sodium yellow glow rose from the horizon, but the sky was black and cloudless.

Lucy stopped near the centre of the clearing and said, "Which way's North-East?"

John's sense of direction was always good on roads and in streets, but he rarely thought in terms of compass points. He had a slight recollection that the evening sun shone onto the stage door at this venue. Mentally he worked out the direction of the theatre from where they stood and rotated to North-East from where he guessed West to be. "Maybe about there," he said, pointing.
Lucy turned him to face that way, and stood in front of him, leaning back against him with her head tilted back to rest on his chest so she was looking up at the sky. He put on foot a half pace back to brace against her weight and rested his hands on her shoulders. She was so much shorter than him that she was below his chin if he looked up at the night sky.

For a very long time they saw nothing except for the red and white lights of a distant plane crossing from right to left in front of them very high up. John rubbed his thumbs gently across her shoulders, smoothing the material of her stage black shirt where it was rucked by her bra straps.

Suddenly she said, "Look!" and by chance he was looking near enough to the direction she was to see a momentary tiny streak of white light almost straight ahead of them.

"Did you make a wish?" she asked, turning excitedly to him. And he nodded and said "Yes. Did you?"

"Of course," she said, "I wonder if it was the same wish."

On the second night after that they dined more formally, in the hotel dining room. Enough time, and breakfasts, had passed for John to be able to eat there and the scene with Nicole to no longer be at the forefront of his mind, and he welcomed the different surroundings after regular oriental dinners. The atmosphere lulled them both into a warm and cosy mood and they were both eager, when the meal was over, to go up to the room hand in hand.

The bedside phone rang in the cold light of dawn, before the world was properly awake, before the roads had traffic on them and before anyone had any right to be ringing someone else.

John reached for the thing, still half asleep, and grunted, "Yes?"

"Is Lucy there?" an anxious voice asked.

He turned towards her and shook her shoulder gently, saying "It's for you." as he handed her the instrument and tried to stop the cable trailing across his face.

He climbed out of bed. In the pale light he could see that the bedclothes were a tangled mess. Lucy was young and energetic in her love-making. She was struggling to sit up among the twisted sheets, naked limbs sticking out from places where the material had been pulled aside that night. He could hear shock in her voice as she was saying into the receiver, "No!" and "When?" and "Not her!" and eventually "I'll be there at once."

She rolled onto her front to reach out to put the phone back on the bedside table. Then she scrambled off the bed, sheets trailing, and lunged at him, pounding at his bare chest with balled fists and screaming "You bastard!" Her hair, tousled from the night and her violent attack on him, hung across her face so half of it was obscured.

He grabbed her wrists to stop her blows, and tried to quieten her by making shushing noises. He was concerned about the neighbouring hotel bedrooms as much as he was trying to discover what had upset her. They swayed together by the bed with the tangled bedding sliding down to the floor. He was aware of her body next to him even while attempting to discover what she was angry about.

"You set it up you bastard! You planned it all with that bloody woman. Now she's ransacking Bill's house!"

"What do you mean?"

"The police are there... they've broken the door down and they're tearing his house apart, and that Moira is in charge of them. And you set it up, I heard the two of you. She said she could sort some timings or something, so you wouldn't be involved, and you pretended to shout at her and... Oh god I don't know!" and she wept.

Still confused John hugged her, and asked, "Do you want to go to Bill's house?"

She nodded.

"Get dressed then," and he picked up the phone and called reception, ordering a taxi at once.

As soon as they were both dressed they went downstairs. They were asked if they wanted breakfast, but said 'no' and went outside to await the cab. It was chill in the early morning, and she had only thrown on jeans and a tee shirt. She was trying to comb her hair, but the tangles were causing her to wrench at it in stuccato jerks. He hung his jacket round her shoulders, took the comb from her hand and began a more gentle, and ultimately effective, combing.

She was still cursing and blaming him. He was still unsure what exactly had happened. The cab arrived. They got in and she gave the address and said to the driver, "Quickly, quickly!"

On the way he tried again to assure her that this raid was nothing to do with him, but she kept insisting that it was all his fault.

The morning rush hour in the city had hardly begun, and the short journey meant that the driver soon turned into the road that led up to Bill and Alison's home.

"It doesn't look as if I can get much further," the driver said, over his shoulder. And he was right, for a seeming mass of police vehicles, with blue lights flashing, was clustered around Bill's house, blocking the road.

House doors were open on both sides of the street with curious neighbours, some still in dressing gowns, in their doorways or at their garden gates.

John thanked, and paid the driver, and the two of them ran the remaining few yards. They were stopped by a uniformed policeman. He held a hand up, and said flatly, "You can't go along here."

"That's my brother's house!" shouted Lucy.

A female officer, clad in uniform, with protective vest and a pseudo military look turned from near the garden path. It was Moira.

"Moira! What the hell is going on?" John demanded loudly.

"Stay out of this," she told him.

"Rubbish," he said, and marched straight toward her, "What on earth are you and your gang playing at?"

The uniformed policeman put a hand in the middle of John's chest as if to stop him, but John brushed him aside, noticing as he did so that the officer was no more than a calow youth.

"Now then sir, that's assaulting a police officer," the youngster said.

"Oh grow up!" John told him, and carried on.

Moira said, "It's all right. I'll deal with this." and in a second John, and Lucy who had followed him, were beside Moira at the garden gate. Moira glowered at him, "I told you to steer clear of this."

"And what exactly is this?"

"We have reason to believe that drugs are being dealt from this house..."

"Bill would never have anything to do with drugs," Lucy butted in.

"I give you fair warning," Moira turned her attention to Lucy and adopted her hard tone, "we will be asking you some serious questions when we find anything."

"Where's my family?" Lucy wanted to know.

But at that moment a small knot of police came out through the front door. John saw now that the door had been smashed, and the lock hung by a splintered strip of timber. The leading policeman had a dog with him, he came straight to Moira and shook his head.

"Nothing?" she asked him.

"Not a thing. Bad guess this time."

Lucy and John both started to berate Moira.

"Where's my family?" she demanded again. "What are you going to do about the damage you've caused?" John wanted to know.

"We will secure the property..."

"But not mend the damage?"

"... and no further charges will be brought..."

"There shouldn't have been any charges in the first place. What about compensation?"

Moira turned on her heel and wallked away.

Tentatively Lucy and John went to the front door. Inside the empty house was a shambles. Every cupboard door was open, drawers were tipped out, the family's possessions were strewn across the floors, many smashed. It was as if a rampaging herd of elephants had entered the house.

Lucy uttered a faint "Oh no!" and sank onto the settee and began to cry again.

John picked up the phone and started to dial from memory. Where she sat the girl heard snatches of the conversation;

"Yes I know it's early...." and then some explanation of the situation, then "The best bloke you've got locally... well I think you owe it to me... no, at once... At the local nick I think..."

There was a lot of discussion, but it ended with, "Thank you Levi, and we'll see you later."

He went over to Lucy. She looked up at him through damp eyes. "What's happening?"

"Levi is aranging his best local legal people, and believe me if Levi uses them they will be very good, to go to the police station at once and get your family out of there. But he's pretty sure the police don't accept any liability for damage on occasions like these.."

She gasped, looked about, and said "Oh no!"

"... but he's sorting repair workers, and he's agreed to pay for the replacement of anything that's been broken. He's driving straight here from London, and calling a meeting of everyone involved during this afternoon. Trust me when I say if he says these things will get sorted out they will, and immediately."

Lucy didn't know whether to thank John or carry on blaming him. They went outside. The collection of police cars had vanished, leaving just one parked across the gateway, and a single uniformed poiceman guarding the wrecked front door. The neighbours had mostly withdrawn back into their houses for breakfast, though further up the road two curious onlookers still stood on their steps watching with evident disapproval on their faces.

John said to him, "We would offer you a cup of tea, but your friends seem to have managed to smash everything."

He was met with a stolid silence, and he had the impression that this copper had been told to keep his mouth shut. The moment dragged, but suddenly a builder's van swept into the street and came to a halt outside.

"You were quick!" John said to the man who got out.

"Do you know Mr Fisher?" said the workman, "When he says now, he means 'now'. Especially when its quadruple time rates," he added thoughtfully. And he immediately started working on the front door.

"Did he say quad time?" Lucy asked, disbelievingly.

John nodded. "I wanted to try to get things under way before your brother and his family get back.

Lucy was still angry with John, still not certain whether the raid on her brother's home had been in some way connected to his having Moira as an assistant, still upset by what she had seen at the house, and now bemused by the speed with which John seemed to be arranging repairs. It didn't stop her confused ideas about him being in some way responsible, but she had to admit gratitude, for she would not have known where to begin.

"I suppose I ought to try to clear the mess up in there," she said.

"Come on then." They scrambled past the workman at the front door and went back in. Lucy stood helplessly surveying the kitchen, the lounge, and suddenly saying "What is it like upstairs do you think?"

The climbed the narrow staircase. The contents of the airing cupboard on the landing were spilt onto the floor. In the main bedroom, Bill and Alison's room, drawers hung open, garments were scattered. The back bedroom was obviously the boy's room, and young Bill had decorated it with football posters. It was hard to tell how much of the mess was due to the police and how much was normal. The hatch to the loft hung open, dangling on its hinges ready for the unwary to bang their head on it.

Emily had been given the small box room, and the collection of girly cuddly toys had been swept aside and cupboards emptied.

The bathroom exhibited similar rough searching and some smashed bottles.

"I think you'd better have a go at the bedrooms," John said, "I don't think your family would want any more strangers handling their clothes. I'll make a start downstairs."

121

Nearly an hour later Lucy came down, finding him in the kitchen re-stacking crockery.

"I hope I've guessed where things go correctly," he said.

"It looks much better anyway," she conceded, "Why did they have to make such a mess?"

"Bloody self importance, that's why," he said. Lucy's labouring clearing up in the bedrooms had made her sad. John had found his antagonism toward Moira and anger at the police had grown with every minute. He might have carried on whipping himself up into ever more self righteous fury over it all now, had a police car not pulled up outside and disgorged Bill, Alison and Emily. A second car was moments behind with young Bill accompanied by a police woman.

Emily ran to Lucy, tear stained and yelling "Auntie Lucy! They broke my theatre!"

Lucy hugged the child. "Never mind, we'll get you another one," she looked meaningly at John, who nodded. Emily raised her head from where it was buried in Lucy's front, looked at John, and, with the naïvity of childhood asked, "Are you my Uncle John now?"

"What makes you say that?" Lucy asked her.

"When the nasty men came mummy said she'd got to ring you, and daddy said you'd be with Uncle John at his hotel and no-one had got up by then, so.."

"Yes, yes. Don't you worry about it," Lucy interrupted the child.

John was trying not to laugh, despite the situation. 'Out of the mouths of babes...' he thought.

Lucy gave him a stern look and hissed at him, "And I don't know at the moment, I'm still very annoyed with you for causing all this!"

Emily had heard, of course, and said, "You do love each other don't you?"

They were saved from any more embarassing and, in Lucy's case uncertain, questions by young Bill kicking a football against the wooden fence furiously in an evident temper. Alison was trying to calm him, but the morning's events had affected him, perhaps more than they had his sister, who seemed to have recovered her talkative nature quite quickly.

"Bill's cross because he thinks he'll miss football practice this afternoon," she told them.

"I'm sure he'll be able to go this afternoon,"

"Of course he will," Bill agreed with his wife, and put his hand on the boy's shoulder to try to calm the vicious kicking of each rebound from the fence. The boy shook his father's hand off and stamped into the house.

"It's upset us all," Bill told his sister, "Who's that working on the door?"

"Levi, my boss, is sorting out all the repairs for you," John explained, noting that although Bill and Alison said 'thank you' they did so in a subdued and resentful way.

Alison went into the house. She returned immediately saying, "Who cleaned up?"

"We did a bit of tidying," Lucy told her, "I hope we put things in the right places."

"Thanks sis," Bill said, "we were dreading it. Anything will have helped. They were so violent. They smashed their way in screaming and shouting. They were yelling all the time as if we were armed criminals." He stopped. Then he said very quietly to Lucy, "I thought they might be one of the London gangs. I was really frightened. I didn't know if Dad had got into some trouble."

Chapter 12

Levi had taken the suite at the top of the hotel that John was stopping in. John and Lucy had gone back to their room to wash and change before taking the lift to the suite in obedient response to the impressario's summons to a meeting in the middle of the afternoon.

Lucy was still being a little stand-offish with John, still unable to convince herself that his bringing Moira into the 'Chuzzlewit' company wasn't in some way the cause of her family's distressing experience that morning. Logically she knew it couldn't have been something he deliberately arranged, but she needed someone from outside to convince her, and she hadn't found that someone yet.

The suite was everything you'd have expected. A large, tastefully decorated, living room with two settees, four armchairs, a dining table with four chairs around it, drinks cabinets, coffee tables; it was like a very plush apartment in its own right. Doors off the room presumably led to bedroom, bathroom and a kitchen.

Levi was ensconced in an armchair at one end of the room with his back to the big windows. You could see rooftops outside, but the bright afternoon sun made it hard to get a good look at Levi's expression against the light. John decided that his boss might have carefully staged the layout for this meeting.

Three other people were already in the room. John knew Janice, Levi's secretary, who was answering the door as people knocked, and ushering them in. It was unusual for her to travel out of the head office. John couldn't remember a previous occasion when she had come to a city on the touring route for any show.

He recognised Levi's regular solicitor, who had taken one of the dining chairs as far away from the centre of the room as possible, and had spread a few documents on the slippery, shiny polished surface of the table.

Frank had one of the armchairs and was lounging in it with a leg dangling over one of the arms. He seemed to be putting on a deliberate stance of nonchallence.

John and Lucy took one of the settees facing Levi. Levi's bonhomie seemed to be in abeyance and there was no small talk beyond rather curt 'hello's. Another knock as they settled themselves and Moira came in, accompanied by a cross looking man in a cheap suit, obviously from the police. They took armchairs.

Levi looked at his watch.

"We're missing one more person," he said, "we'll wait a few moments."

No-one spoke, and some thirty seconds dragged by very slowly. John studied the décor and decided it was the wrong shade of peach, bordering on pink, which gave the room a feminine feel, unsuited to what might well become a confrontational meeting. He rehearsed his gripes in his mind, resolving again that he would have his say, and to hell with the consequences. He would be vocal in his criticism of having had Moira foisted on him and of her behaviour. He would defend Lucy's family, even though Levi had pulled out all the stops in terms of reparations. He squeezed Lucy's hand and she looked at him rather severely, but she didn't pull her hand away.

A timid knock came at the door and Janice opened it. John looked back over his shoulder and was surprised. Nicole was probably the last person he had expected Levi to summon here this afternoon. She was ushered in, and she sat perched on the edge of one of the dining chairs. Now Lucy tried to catch John's eye, but sat side by side on a settee this was difficult. Like John she was at a loss as to why Nicole was there, and all her jealous feelings welled up again. For John to parade his ex at this meeting about her family's disruption and mal-treatment seemed like a slap in the face.

"Why?" she whispered to John.

"I don't know, it's a surprise to me," he whispered back.

Levi tapped a glass beside him as if having to call a rowdy crowd to order. John noticed, and mourned the fact, that they hadn't been offered any drinks. He felt the need of a good shot of whisky.

"I've called you to try to sort out this ridiculous situation," Levi started, "If anyone is to blame it may be me, but I was put into a situation which I didn't like, and was given no choice by some very authoritarian bullies."

The suited man with Moira coughed slightly as if he was about to interrupt, but Levi held up his hand like a copper directing traffic, and the impresario's presence meant he kept command.

"I'm sure you've worked out what was going on, Miss Wade, please bear with us you'll get the drift as we discuss it. Moira was foisted on the 'Chuzzlewit' company as a spy, there is not a kinder word. According to the police, and in case you hadn't realised, she's a cop, it was essential she should be on the road with the show. I argued with them but they made very serious threats that might have affected the production and I had to give in. Worse I had to mislead you, John. If you thought John was in on it, you're wrong, He was probably the biggest victim, forced to accept an incompetent woman without knowing why."

Frank said bluntly, "Why?"

"The cops claim.."

"It's not a claim, its a fact!" Moira cut in.

Levi fixed her with a frown and then carried on as if she had not spoken, "The cops claim that drugs are being shipped around the country, using my show as a mule. They claim that the local market has a sudden burst of extra stock every time 'Chuzzlewit' arrives in any city. They claim that new dealers appear on the streets within a few days of us opening. It's happened twice I'm told. Barely more than a coincidence I'd have thought. I was compelled to bring Moira into the company so she could snoop about and try to catch whoever it was."

Some slow understanding came to his stage manager and company manager.

"I never gave permission for that woman," Levi pointed at Moira, "to disrupt my show or organise raids on people working for my show. I'm pleased to say that she's blown her own cover and will not be with you any more."

Moira spoke up, "We had ample evidence to raid the Gainsborough's house today. We'd had the dogs into the theatre in the first twenty-four hours in this city, and they found nothing, so the drugs had to have left already, and the only regular shipments out of the building were costumes going to laundry. What better than boxes of soap powder to hide drugs in. We'd done a discreet sniff at the laudrette with the dogs and turned up a blank, so the gear had to be at Bill Gainsborough's house."

"Except it wasn't," Levi said coldly.

"We still think it had already been moved on. And that's another reason she," Moira pointed at Lucy, "shouldn't be here. I told you that! She and her brother have gangland connections through their father."

At the table Levi's solicitor made a note.

"That might be slander," Levi looked at the solicitor, who made a side to side 'maybe' motion with his head, "Anyway I will have exactly who I like at a meeting I call."

Moira interrupted him, "This drug traffic has to be stopped.."

"I'm quite sure that's true. But you're not using this company again. None-the-less I've agreed with your boss," the suited copper shrugged at being mentioned, "that we will privately seek out any dealing that is going on and inform the cops in whatever city we are in when, or if, we learn anything."

"If your amateur sleuthing disrupts an official enquiry we will charge you with obstructing the police." Moira was unabashed at her error and forcefully standing her ground.

"Granted," said Levi, "and my solicitors will be issuing claims for damages tomorrow."

"That will do you no good. We have the right..."

John had seen Levi in all sorts of moods. He'd seen him in bad temper before. But he had never seen him so determined and commanding. John had to admire the man's confidence which seemed to enable him to berate the police presence with some impunity. The vaneer of Jewish obsequiousness had vanished. True Levi's solicitor was there, but to John it spoke volumes about the man's power.

"I would have hoped," Levi cut across Moira's words as if there had been no interruption, "that the police would have been keen to supply us with any information they might have, to assist the theatre company in tracing any criminal that might be among them. Not that we think there is. But they've refused to help at all. We will just have to see what we can do without them, because in the interests of good will and public co-operation I have decided we will look into this and wrap it up one way or another. If one of my staff is indulging in criminal activity I want to know," he paused and surveyed the gathering. They sat silently. "If we are all, as I'm sure we are, completely innocent I will expect recompence and apologies."

The suited policeman rose to his feet. "There's not much else to say then if that's your attitude," he declared, "Your interference threatens the investigation and we will take advice about that, but we can't really stop you playing amateur sleuths."

Moira said to him, "You're going to let them?" in a shocked tone.

"We don't seem to have much choice. Come on." and he left with Moira trailing in his wake and slamming the door behind her.

Levi let out a long breath and said, "Well that's made for a better atmosphere."

Faintly Nicole asked, "Why am I here?" she had been confused by Levi's demand that she come to the meeting, a bit surprised at what she had gathered from what had been said, and overridingly she had been upset at what she saw as the way John and Lucy were seated together. Her fears about their relationship were confirmed and she wondered if Levi was making the situation blatantly apparent to her as a means of warning her off so as to protect John's state of mind.

Levi smiled at her saying, "Miss Wade, you are my essential secret weapon in the bit of amateur detective work we are about to undertake. The force felt it necessary to secrete a mole in the company's midst. It didn't work, but the plan may have been sound. We will do the same, and don't worry, you will get paid for your time," her face brightened slightly, "and if it all goes well I think we can be sure there will be a part for you to play somewhere in the Levi Fischer empire."

Nicole felt a little burst of hope. Hope of employment, for there had been no sign of work elsewhere, and hope of being close to John.

"Miss Gainsborough," said Levi, "tell us about this morning. I want my solicitor to hear it first hand."

"Well, my brother's house was raided very early. They broke the door down and made a big mess, smashing things and emptying cupboards and drawers. By the time we got there..."

"You went to the house?" She nodded. "How did you know that something was happening?"

"Alison, my sister in law, rang John's hotel, and he passed the phone to me."

Nicole gave an involuntary gasp and put her hand to her mouth to stifle it. Her fear was confirmed. John looked with some sad pity at Nicole, and Levi surveyed both of them like a hawk, carefully assessing the relationships. "Go on," he said.

"We got a taxi and went straight round there. The street was full of blue lights, but just as we arrived the cops seem to decide that there was nothing there. They'd taken the family away."

"The family?"

"Bill and Alison, and young Bill and Emily, their children."

The solicitor made more notes nodding to Levi when he had finished..

"And eventually they brought them back?"

"Yes. We tried to clean the place up before they came back, but it was such a mess, and there were so many things broken."

Levi looked sympathetic. "I've promised to buy replacements for anything that was damaged."

"You can't replace things with sentimental value," Lucy mumbled looking down at the carpet.

"No, I'm sorry, I can't."

"What about me? What have I got to do?" Nicole asked, now a

little unsure how she felt about being close to John again having had his relationship with Lucy confirmed.

"Half the 'Chuzzlewit' company knows that you were once with John," Levi looked to them for confirmation, but got no firm encouragement, "If they think you two are back together you'll be able to come and go backstage, and no-one will pay any attention. So you, John and Miss Gainsborough can compare notes."

"But John and I... No forget it." said Lucy angrily.

John finally spoke, "If the word gets round that I've ditched Lucy there will be all sorts of bad feeling, not least from wardrobe and.."

"Who says it's you ditching me?"

Lucy's sudden vehemence startled John. Once he had been sorry for Nicole and her insecurities, now he began to feel he knew how she must feel.

"Go away and work out a scenario that you can live with. I don't care what it is, but this is how we are going to do this."

The three of them flinched at the command. John said, "Can we take some people into our confidence, like Brenda and Alice?"

"Brenda and Alice?"

"Wardrobe. It would make Lucy's life easier."

"Yes, I know Brenda."

Nicole thought that John seemed more concerned about Lucy's life than how the situation might affect her. Was she to pretend to be in a relationship with him, or would she really be? She couldn't quite make her mind up whether she wanted to pretend to be John's girlfriend again, or actually be. And the little exchange between John and Lucy had confirmed that not only were they together, and sleeping in his hotel room, but that the whole company knew it. The hotel room that she had shared with him just a few days ago. She was sensitive enough to have detected a sharp edge to Lucy's 'who says you're ditching me?' comment, and thought, hoped perhaps, that there might have been friction there before Levi put them in this impossible scenario.

Levi said, "Do what you think best, John. You will anyway, whatever I say, but remember, if there's a drug dealer in our midst I want him found and charged, and if there isn't I want you to have been thorough enough that we can get these coppers off our back for good."

Levi rose. It was obviously a dismissal. Like school children when a master entered a room the group stood too, slowly heading for the door. John was last out, standing aside to allow Nicole through, and he turned to look over his shoulder at Levi. The solicitor and Janice were collecting papers and shutting brief cases.

"I don't like all this."

"One day, my boy, we will look back at it and laugh, trust me. Oh, and don't bother about a comp for tonight, I'm going straight back to town."

John nodded, thinking what a shame it was to waste the luxurious suite. Fleetingly he wondered if he could comandeer it for the night, then found himself unsure as to who he might be able to share it with. Lucy needed some serious care and attention as a result of the raid and all the family upset of that morning, and Nicole... well he'd assumed that what had happened between them had been just a fling, a nod to their previous relationship, and not the start of a serious return to being a couple. Now Levi had put confusion on top of delicate relations by telling them to act parts that none of them were sure if they actually wanted.

He shut the door. Lucy, Nicole and Frank were standing by the lift waiting for him.

Frank said, "If I read the situation correctly Levi has just handed you a dilemma, wrapped in an enigma with two explosive packages attached," he nodded toward Lucy and Nicole.

John looked at his watch. "We need to sit down and thrash this out. If we went to my room now we've got some time before any of us need to be at the theatre. Lucy, how possible would it be for both Brenda and Alice to get away for an hour or so at this point in the afternoon?"

"They'll say its impossible, but so long as there's no major repair jobs, and I don't think any were mentioned after last night's show, it should be OK."

"Could you go and fetch them, please. Try not to say too much about it all in the theatre, of course, just what you need to get them here. We'll wait."

Lucy seemed a bit annoyed at being made to be a messenger, but actually it was because she saw that this would mean Nicole and John would be together. Oh, Frank would be there, but John could easily think of an errand for him, she decided. She set off, determined to be as quick as she could.

Chapter 13

In John's room Frank and Nicole watched as he rang for room service and ordered plates of sandwiches, teas and coffees, and what seemed a very large quantity of spirits.

"John, that's a lot of alcohol." Nicole protested when he hung up.

"Don't worry, I expect I can manage it." he told her grimly, and before the hotel had even begun to make the food and deliver it he took a miniature whisky out of the bar and poured it for himself. He felt he deserved it. "Anyone else while we're waiting?" he asked.

Frank and Nicole shook their heads.

'It's become a crutch,' Nicole thought sadly, 'anything that comes along now, ever since Penelope died, I suppose, he goes straight to the bottle.'

"Frank summed this up rather well didn't he?" he said perching on the desk and knocking back the scotch. "I hadn't realised you were so clued up on my relationships, Frank," he addressed Nicole, "What do you want to happen?"

"I want it all to go away," she said sadly, "I thought.. well I didn't know you'd hitched up with Lucy as soon as we'd, you know. And I don't think I can act being with you. If I don't do it convincingly it will look silly, and if I put in a good performance Lucy won't know whether to be jealous or not, and if I'm acting it... John I'll be wanting it to be real, I know I said 'just one night' but you know I will."

Frank, his suspicions confimed, said, "You three are going to have to work this one out yourselves. Include me out."

From his perch on the desk John had seen that, although the hotel had made up the room it still showed some signs of his and

Lucy's occupancy. Some of her underwear had been neatly folded and placed on the bedside table and her rather skimpy dressing gown hung in view on a hook in the bathroom, the door to which stood open. He got up and tidied these items away into drawers.

Nicole said, "We've been here before haven't we, John? You and me, and you wanting someone else."

"Last time you wanted someone else too."

"We'll just have to pretend that's still the case," she said, bravely.

There was a knock at the door, and the food and drink was delivered. It had arrived on a trolley, which was lucky as there certainly weren't enough spare surfaces to put things down. John thanked the girl, and Nicole noticed him slipping some cash into her hand.

Frank studied the trolley. "Can we start our picnic then?"

"Let's wait for the others," said John, but he opened a bottle of whisky that was among the drinks and refilled his glass.

They didn't have long to wait. Lucy arrived with Brenda and Alice. All three were slightly breathless from hurrying through the streets. Brenda combined this with obvious annoyance.

"I hope this is worth dragging us away from washing and ironing. We were already behind because Lucy's brother couldn't do the stuff that we've been farming out to him," she looked around the room, "Some people are clearly being paid too much," she added bitterly.

John ignored the barbed comment.

"Sit down all of you, help yourselves to food and drink," he told them, and then launched into a succinct explanation of the day's events and Levi's dealing with the situation, finishing with Levi's instructions about how they were to proceed.

"So you see that not only have we become a sort of unofficial detective agency, with strict orders to find the culprit, if there is one, he's also put us in a position which is.. well delicate and embarassing."

"Only for you perhaps," said Brenda. She was fond of John, but was more concerned by what she'd just heard about the day's upset for Lucy's family, and Lucy.

"For me. For Nicole," he gestured in her direction, "who really had no connection with the 'Chuzzlewit' company till this morning..."

"Except for you two-timing Lucy with her," Brenda interrupted.

"..and for Lucy."

"I think we have to be blunt and honest," Brenda said, "does Nicole want to be your girlfriend, does Lucy still want to be your girlfriend, and which one do you want to be your girlfriend? It's a simple question."

It didn't seem a simple question to John. Frank started handing round the sandwiches quietly.

There was silence, till Lucy said, "I got really cross with John this morning because I thought that he'd arranged the raid with Moira. I understand now it wasn't his fault... I think I might be able to forgive him, but I think he still fancies Nicole. She was with you once wasn't she?"

Nicole nodded, and with more confidence than usual said, "Yes, we were together, and yes I still fancy him."

John thought, 'Did she have to say that she still fancied me?'

Brenda looked at John. "Come on John, tell us, honestly."

John found himself the centre of curiosity from every pair of eyes in the room. He'd never had to make a public announcement of this sort. If he confessed the lingering liking for, and pity of, Nicole it would certainly bring any fledgling affair with Lucy crashing down. If he confessed his strong desire for the wardrobe girl it would be a slap in the face for the actress, and probably brutal for her confidence. He had dumped her once before, and it had only been her infatuation with Laurence that had meant she hadn't been very upset. Levi's instructions had produced extra complications, for, although he thought that he could give an outward appearance of carrying on with Nicole with only some private frustration, he lacked faith in her ability to act that part. In any case Lucy had already displayed jealousy, and she would be required to act the role of one jilted. Could she carry that off? And would she trust him that it was just an act with Nicole?

"It's going to be a problem," he admitted. "Nicole and I had already agreed that it was over between us," he watched Nicole's reaction, and was unsurprised when she nodded, but sniffed sadly. "She and I could maybe act the roles that Levi's demanding, but I think Lucy's already upset at me, and she'd have to be pretending to have been ditched....... and I don't want to ditch Lucy," he blurted out at the end.

Alice gave an interrogative look at Brenda and spoke for the first time. "I don't see why Lucy has to be dumped, unless she wants to be of course."

Lucy could be seen slowly shaking her head.

"Well, I just thought, if Levi is simply looking for an excuse for Nicole to be backstage why can't she pretend to pair up with Frank? She'd be expected to go in and out of the same dressing room, I mean office, and Lucy wouldn't have to put up with a lot of sympathy from the cast all the time as she goes round with costumes and things."

John thought it was the longest speech he'd ever heard Alice make.

Brenda said, "That's brilliant. And no! Don't you dare say you need to check it with Levi. We'll do that, and he can like it or lump it. I can deal with Levi if he argues."

"Anyone going to ask me or Nicole then?" said Frank.

"I'd be happy to pretend to be your girlfriend, Frank," said Nicole. Then with a return to her normal uncertainty, "if you wouldn't mind?"

"Of course I wouldn't mind. Though the cast are going to think it's strange me getting the pretty girl instead of John."

John grabbed a sandwich and poured himself another whisky. "Would you be happy with Alice's idea, Lucy?" he asked.

Lucy nodded and said, "Please don't drink so much, John."

He emptied the glass and stood it down. Still holding the sandwich he looked at his watch, stopping to rub the scar as he did so.

"OK, just time to work out what we're going to do then," he said.

"Oh, that's simple," Brenda said, sarcastically, "as we go round the cast we just ask each one if they are drug dealers. And I bet none of them are."

Alice said, "We'll have to get to socialise with them all and bring drugs into the conversation and watch for reactions."

"What am I supposed to do then?" asked Nicole.

"You, darling, are the distraction," said Frank, "just mingle and distract, but keep your ears open."

John felt a moment's envy at how quickly Frank was using endearments. 'Darling' was an overused word backstage, but Frank didn't usually include it in his vocabulary. Lucy must have seen some expression, because she grabbed his hand and whispered, "Hey! You're with me remember!"

"We'll meet up every so often and compare notes," said Brenda, "I suggest wardrobe. We've all got an excuse to be there, well except Nicole of course, but she can come with Frank, and someone can just keep an eye on the corridor to make sure no-one is coming."

John realised that the whole undercover operation was being taken out of his hands, and was secretly glad. "Right, back to the theatre," he said.

They left, taking food from the trolley as they went. Soon only John and Lucy remained. She faced him and took both his hands in hers. "I'm sorry I was suspicious this morning."

"You had every right to be," he told her.

"Hey!" she said suddenly, "Where's my clothes and things?"

"I didn't think you'd want everyone seeing them lying about, they're in that drawer, and your dressing gown too, it was hanging in there," he pointed.

"You do think of everything. It's really sweet."

Chapter 14

Nicole was accepted into the 'Chuzzlewit' family with surprisingly little comment. Many of the cast were quietly pleased on Frank's behalf, solitary members of cast and crew were often the objects of wannabe matchmakers attentions, and as Nicole was both an actress, and had links to the company from her previous fling with John there was no sense of anyone wondering how she'd met Frank.

The company had also accepted John and Lucy as a couple, although John constantly felt he was walking a tight-rope with her in their relationship. She was much more independent than Nicole had ever been; more likely to express a forthright opinion, and the very recent history of the family's being under such suspicion had caused an element of distrust which had not been there at the start. Lucy knew and now accepted that John had not been responsible, but some doubts about Nicole still lingered in her mind.

Two days after the police raid Lucy went to work in wardrobe as usual, but John didn't go with her, saying he had some errands to run. That morning found him in the city's major department store, prowling the toy section. After long searching, some hunting through catalogues with the staff, and negotiations over deliveries, he left the store, poorer, but pleased that he had done his best.

He arrived at the stage-door at the same time as Elaine, 'Mollie's Garden's ASM. He held the door for her. He saw that he had been right about her appearance: cropped hair, no make-up, mannish heavy working boots and dungarees over a check shirt. She had no discernable figure in this outfit and the rather flat front of the dungarees was liberally plastered with numerous badges. He found he couldn't avoid reading them as they went up in the lift. Equally he was sure that she was about to comment. There were badges for rock bands, for theatre companies and for a few famous festivals, as well as political slogans. He thought he'd pre-

141

empt any criticism of where he was looking.

"That's an impressive collection of badges."

She shrugged, and the lift jerked to a halt at the first floor, the doors rattling open to let them out.

"A girl's got to have a hobby," she said as they walked along the passage together. He laughed.

"Any other hobbies?"

"Is that a chat-up line?"

He hesitated how to say 'no, absolutely not,' without being insulting, and was saved by arriving at the company office door. Instead he said, "This is where I get off," and dived into his room.

He heard the next door along slam as Elaine went into the kids' show production office. Almost immediately a quick knock at his door heralded Lucy, who had obviously been watching out for his arrival from the wardrobe room. She came over and kissed him as if she hadn't seen him for ages, rather than just that morning.

"Were you chatting up that woman from the kids' show?" she asked coquettishly.

"Heavens, no! What an awful thought," he answered.

"The others all think we should have a get together to sort out how we are going to do this detecting," she told him, dropping the flippant discussion of Elaine, "We thought this afternoon, about tea-time, maybe in here, rather than wardrobe. We could all still have a good excuse for being here, no-one would be surprised."

He agreed, saying "Spread the word," and shooing her out with a peck on the cheek.

So it was that while 'Mollie's Garden' played to another packed house of squealing infants the amateur sleuths crowded into his office to thrash out tactics. They all reported that in their own ways they had kept their ears to the ground since Levi had ordered them to play this role. They also had to admit that none of them had caught the slightest hint of any dealing within the company. Nicole said that she'd made discreet enquiries outside the confines of the theatre, also without success.

"I suppose we could go out onto street corners and see if we could buy any drugs and who from," Alice said tentatively. John thought that was a bad idea.

Brenda was emphatic again that she had seen no sign of drugs in all her tramping from dressing room to dressing room.

It was Frank who suggested a ploy. "You see," he said, "it could take for ever for one of us to happen across an incriminating conversation by random chance, which is pretty much what we are banking on. If we could get the whole cast and crew together for some reason, sort of socially, we might be able to mingle and listen."

John thought and then said, "We're close to the two-hundred and fiftieth performance aren't we?"

"Due late next week I think," said Frank, "Are you thinking we should have a party?"

"I think exactly that," John said, "A big get together for everyone here in the theatre somewhere after the show."

"Will the house management let us do that?" Brenda wondered.

"I'll have a word with them. If we had one of the upstairs bars through into the early hours it would be a good long time for everyone to be together and drinks to loosen tongues."

"Not too much drink," a worried Lucy said to him.

They checked on the date of the landmark performance, allocated minor organisational roles for themselves, and John set off to talk to house management about using a front of house bar after the show that particular evening.

Chapter 15

The company was eager in its anticipation of the party. A small cabaret was being arranged starring a few of the cast and some of the musicians, there were many offers of food, and best of all John had persuaded Levi to foot a very generous bar bill, much to the delight of the House Manager, who was arranging for some of his staff to serve overtime that night at the function which everyone expected to last well into the early hours.

Performances ran as usual, like clockwork, but as the special night approached John noticed a number of changes to routine among his company. The daily vocal warm-up session, on stage before the half, taken by the musical director, was starting a few minutes earlier, and now included some numbers that were not in the show being sung. Intrigued, he wandered out front through the pass door one day, and leant on the orchestra pit rail. Some of the minor members of the cast were clearly rehearsing, he assumed this was the promised cabaret.

In his own corridor an unusual noise could be heard. It was the sound of a sewing machine being driven swiftly through material. It came from wardrobe. He recognised that it was a rare noise, because with a show that was established it was only very occasional repairs that would be major enough to involve a sewing machine, although the company carried them. This activity seemed to be making rather than mending. He asked Lucy as they sat in bed one night.

"Can't keep anything secret from you can we," she replied.

"Don't tell me, let me guess... Brenda's found an old wardrobe skip to use as the basket and has got you sewing up a hot air balloon to go with it because that's going to be her new Sunday hobby."

"Correct. Got it in one. Or you could have guessed costumes for the cabaret at the after show on Saturday night."

He humphed. "Have I got to lose the material costs into the budgets somehow, or are we looking at another unexpected burst of Levi generosity?"

"Brenda said that she'd had a word with him and he had told her to spend whatever she needed to."

"Really?" He knew Levi had been generous, almost reckless, in passing expenditure lately, now he'd found another bit of spending that was quite out of character.

He questioned the entrepreneur the following day when they spoke on the phone.

"You've not turned up a criminal for me yet, my boy," his boss said, "I think the party idea is very good. I hear that was you."

"Well it was Frank really," John said modestly.

"Whoever it was I think it's worth throwing some bread on the waters to see if we can catch anything."

"And if we don't?"

"Obviously I shall expect you to re-imburse me from your wages, my boy."

"Thank you, Levi, you're a real gent."

Later Lucy stopped at the office on one of her trips to and from wardrobe.

"That was very generous of you, John," she said.

He looked puzzled, momentarily.

"The model theatre."

"Oh it's arrived has it. Good. Does Emily like it?"

"She's over the moon. It got delivered just before she left for school apparently, and Bill and Alison had to almost drag her away from it to go to classes."

"She'd probably have learnt more by playing with it than she will in a classroom."

"Oh you would say that!"

"No, it's true, I mean she's probably going to be thinking about the toy all day instead of listening to some teacher anyway, but there's more education to be had from practical things in general."

Lucy said, "Hum. You might be right, but I wouldn't put that theory to Bill and Alison if I were you. They're both very keen that the kids should get a proper education."

"What a waste of brain cells," he said, only half jokingly.

Late afternoon he was passing through the stage door lobby when he spotted a teenage girl sitting morosely on an old bentwood chair which had been placed incongrouously against one of the vivid red walls. He searched his mind and recalled Irene from the cast asking about digs for her and her daughter on the first day in the city. This must be the woman's daughter he decided. He remembered something about the girl being a teenager, so the school uniform made sense.

He stopped next to her and said, "Hello."

Her attitude was defiant and he wasn't sure whether she thought he was trying to abduct her or was about to tell her off. He explained who he was. She was unimpressed.

"You must be Irene's daughter," he checked.

The girl gave a grunt that he took to be agreement. "Are the digs all right?" he asked.

Again she was non-commital. "Do you come and stop with your mother every weekend?" he persisted.

"Yeah," then, after a pause, "I'm at boarding school."

John had assumed this would be the case. Weekdays at a boarding school, tedious weekends tied to performances in digs in whatever city the show was in at the time. He wondered about the costs invoved for the girl's mother, comparing his guesses with what he knew her salary as a member of the emsemble cast to be. It didn't leave enough for days out on Sundays, or treats.

"School any good?" he asked, feeling he was interrogating her a bit.

"All right I suppose." she dragged her hair back from her face and tucked it behind her ears and smoothed her uniform skirt across her knees. "We're doing a lot of social studies stuff at the moment."

"What does that involve?" He had no idea what a school might have applied the label to.

"They're on about how social conditions and behaviour affect standards of living," she was opening up, "I don't think they've thought about having a mum in a touring show."

"No, I don't expect they have. What sort of behaviour are they suggesting?"

"Oh, drug taking and things," she said casually.

John pricked up his ears. It occurred to him that this teenager probably knew more about the drugs scene than he and his would-be detectives. Could he pick her brains?

"I don't know much about that," he told her, honestly. Realising he was towering over her by standing he squatted down next to the chair. "What have they told you?"

Predictably the girl had only really absorbed a blanket 'don't' from her teachers. He had hoped to glean some idea of how the marketplace worked, maybe hear some of the street slang. He was very sure that he, Frank, Lucy, Alice, Brenda and Nicole between them had no idea of the language of the streets. He realised that they probably wouldn't even recognise drugs if they saw them. He was pretty sure he wouldn't. He started to turn away, disappointed, when it struck him that Irene probably thought that her child would not be welcome at the forthcoming party, and would therefore miss it herself. It also crossed his mind that a tenager might well be a prime target for a drugs pusher, if there really was one in the company. Maybe a social occasion might draw him or her out.

He said, "Looking forward to the party?"

"Mum said we can't go.. I'm not a member of the company."

"You tell your mum that I said you can. We need some young blood there among all we old dinosaurs," and he rose and went off.

He told the others what he had done when they had one of their councils of war, as Brenda had started calling them, in wardrobe an hour or two later.

"I don't think I'd trust a young girl not to blow our cover," she said.

"I haven't told her anything, just to tell her mother that she can come to the party. We'll have to keep an eye on her and see who talks to her."

"And how the hell are we supposed to watch her all the time in the sort of crowd there will be in a front of house bar at a thing like this?" Alice wanted to know.

"I'm sure that if we are all keeping an eye on her someone would notice if anyone spoke to her," John said.

"You are such a naive idiot, John," said Brenda. "She'll be one of the few strange faces in the crowd. Everyone will speak to her. Oh I don't doubt that the theatre will have a few of its VIPs and big-wigs along, but our villain, if he even exists, will just be one of dozens of people politely saying 'hello' to an out-of-place little girl in a crowd. You don't really think she'd just sit there and no-one would speak to her do you? You spoke to her because she was sitting in the stage door lobby didn't you?"

"Well, yes, when you put it like that. But.."

"It's too late now, we'll have to be even more on the ball, that's all."

The conversation drifted from the group's detective business to the arrangements for the party. John, slightly chastened, and leaning against a washing machine, thought about the reaction to his plan of using the girl as a trap. He was still sure that it might work. Lucy whispered in John's ear, "I think it was a good idea."

He thanked her, and wondered if she was just saying that due to some sort of loyalty.

Chapter 16

Lucy and John sat in the hotel dining room on Saturday morning with the remains of breakfast in front of them. On Lucy's side the white cloth was unmarked, just the plate and an empty cup and saucer before her. John had created a minor tip of toast crumbs and was trying to sweep these up into his hand to empty them back onto a plate.

"What's her name?" Lucy asked.

John looked up confused. Momentarily he thought that Lucy was, once again, suspecting him of two-timing her.

"Irene's daughter. What's her name?"

I haven't the slightest idea," he said, returning to his cleaning up, "but she's only thirteen I think, so it's bound to be something weird and modern like Lucinda or Cassandra."

"I don't know about Lucinda, but Cassandra's not a new name."

"Not 'new', modern. Names go in fashions. People use names that have made the news."

"Name me a Cassandra in the news in the past fifteen years," Lucy challenged him.

"Um. Not news, but wasn't there a Cassandra in a sit-com? Anyway you're right about it being an old name, she was some sort of Greek prophetess."

"The sit-com's much too recent, Cassandra only came into it this year, but I think you're right about prophesy."

He wondered at her certainty about a television programme. Like most of the people in show business he consistently failed to see television unless he recorded it to watch later, and that didn't happen out on the road.

He said, "I remember now, she was cursed so she was always right in her predictions, but no-one ever believed her."

"We'd better believe Irene's daughter if she tells us she's been offered drugs."

"I'm not expecting her to tell us anything, we're just watching."

Lucy stared out of the window, and then said, "John."

"Yes."

"What happens if she is offered some and actually buys them? I mean we might not know if they arranged some drop off point, and then … Well you see."

"I hadn't thought of that. Perhaps Irene will be near enough for that not to happen."

"In which case she's no use to us. You've tied the goat up to lure the monster out. You have to let it take its chance."

"Oh thank you very much for that image!" John was suddenly concerned for the girl.

"Still she wouldn't actually take anything in the middle of a crowd with us all watching..."

"We need to watch everyone," he told her, and finished his table-cloth brushing, took a last swig of the dregs of his tea, grimmaced at it being cold now and stood up saying, "Come on. Time to go to the fun factory."

"Do we really make fun?"

"For the audience, yes. Or at least I hope so. You wouldn't use that nickname for some theatres."

"Or some shows," she ventured, "and I know which ones you'd exclude. In fact," she added cautiously, "I'm not sure I quite get why you think 'Chuzzlewit' is all right when it's based on Dickens. Doesn't that make it a bit high-brow?"

"You can tap your feet to the numbers in 'Chuzzlewit', so I suppose that saves it. But you are right it does teeter on the edge of being a bit worthy for me."

They left the dining room and walked to the Royal. Lucy went to report in to Brenda and John settled to some paperwork. During the morning he was surprised to see Elaine pass his open doorway, going into the 'Mollie's Garden' office. On a Saturday 'Chuzzlewit' had a matinee, so 'Mollie' got a day off. Or was this one of those odd weekends when the management squeezed the kids' show in during the morning? No, he was sure that wasn't the case this week. There was no reason why Elaine shouldn't come in to the theatre even when they were not performing but it intrigued him. The phone rang, stopping any more pondering on his part.

"Hello Levi," he said on answering it, for it could be no-one else.

"Hello, my boy."

John could visualise the other man, reclining in his chair, a generous one, to accommodate the man's generous proportions, a cigar in one hand and the receiver in the other, full of confidence. He wished he felt the same confidence about the coming party that night. His initial feeling that they might 'crack the case' had faded against the criticisms and set backs. It was not like him to be negative or despondent, but that morning, and Lucy's suggestion that he had put the teenager at risk, had dulled his optimism.

"I'm hoping that you are going to reassure me that all the money

153

I'm spending tonight will solve the case."

"Well, there's no guarentees," he told his boss, honestly.

"I prefer it when you give me good news," said Levi.

"I prefer giving you good news, but at the moment the news is that there is no news."

"Don't try to confuse a bamboozler. You've got to get some success from tonight. I'm still fending off the police, but sooner or later someone higher up their chain of command is going to poke their nose in and we'll be back to where we were when they planted that woman on you."

John shook his head in miserable remembrance, distracted only slightly by Elaine leaving the neighbouring office and heading towards the stage door clutching a black case with metal corners under her arm.

Reluctantly he told Levi about his plan to bait the party with Irene's daughter. Levi's reaction was delight. He saw this as a great scheme and was full of praise, "You've come up with another brilliant idea there, my boy," as the idea raised his hopes of drawing a line under the situation. In Levi's eyes an attempt to sell drugs to the child was a win, and the absence of any such attempt proved, to him, at least, that the police information was wrong, and no dealer was darkening their stage door.

John still couldn't see how they were ever to prove a negative. Obviously if they produced a culprit, however inconvenient it turned out to be for the show in terms of their position in cast, crew or orchestra, that would finish the hunt. Failure to find a needle didn't make the haystack innocent in the eyes of authority, and police with a fixed idea in their heads wouldn't just let it drop, he was sure.

He had hardly hung up on Levi when Nicole put her head round the door, saying, "Just going to wardrobe." He nodded distractedly and asked, "No trouble getting past the stage door?"

"Oh no," she assured him, Steve is a sweetie, And now someone has told him Frank and I are," she used both hands to describe inverted commas in the air, "'an item' he doesn't even raise an eyebrow. There's some funny people about though."

"Are there?"

"Who's that butch girl with all the badges?"

"Oh, 'Mollie's Garden's new ASM."

"The kid's show? She came past me with a little flight case looking as if she was guarding the crown jewels," Nicole told him, and went off to meet up with Frank in the wardrobe.

Once the interval of the evening performance had passed there was much additional activity, both backstage, and front of house, and the conclusion of the performance, with its usual standing ovation from the packed audience, saw this activity rise to an almost feverish pitch. Mysterious packages and bundles, musical instruments and amplifiers, costumes and clothes rails all made their way front of house to join the special catering and décor that had been brought to the bar being given over to the party. Front of house had the food and drink well in hand, and the self appointed organisers of the cabaret were arranging the performers and their requirements. John was happy to step back from the coming post-show celebratory performance and give the volunteers free rein. His mind was much more on whether the amateur detectives would be able to report anything, even suspicions, to Levi after this was all over.

The evening performance audience poured out to the exit doors with the exception of the fairly select few who were attending the party as guests. These were waiting on landings for the signal that they could go to the event. There didn't seem to be any annoncement, but somehow the word spread and these people moved en-mass toward the upper circle bar.

John was not among the early arrivers. By the time he did get there the room was quite crowded. Jimmy, the House Manager, was at the door, greeting each arrival with smiles that betrayed his delight at the potential bar sales and the chance of another bit of local press publicity. They were both in evening dress from force of habit. "Hello John," Jimmy said, "Quite a crowd. My bars manager wants to know if you can find any more occasions like this for Levi to subsidise."

"Sadly, no. It's pretty unusual for him to shell out for this sort of thing. He must be doing well from your door sales."
"He drives a hard bargain on the sharing terms deal in the contract.. but it has sold well, we're all doing all right out of it."

"I'm glad to hear it, Jimmy," John told him, and stepped discretely aside as his friend turned to welcome a local supporters' club guest.

Inside a makeshift stage had appeared on an end wall, flanked by two enormous hoarding sized posters for the show, and topped by a cloth banner, clearly painted up by the scenic artists, featuring part of a scene from the show with the letters '250th' superimposed across the centre. A mic and stand were on the platform and several musical instruments and an electric keyboard stood around. John could see that the stores had been raided and some stands carried a few items of stage lighting, dark now, but ready for the cabaret.

He was worried to realise that a crowd such as this, and it was still growing, would be almost impossible to keep any sort of useful observation on, and that any detection was going to rely entirely on mixing and mingling. Sadly he conceded that the critisism of his idea for Irene's daughter to be watched was perfectly valid. Looking around he was at a loss to tell whether she was there yet, and if so where. In the hubub a hand on his arm told him that Lucy had found him. She was looking up at him, smiling happily, her shoulders, bare in the strapless dress she was wearing for the occasion, half hidden by her hair which had clearly been washed and brushed to its silkiest possible condition, and asking why he was looking so glum. He felt a lump in his throat at how attractive she had made herself for this evening while still working two performances and doing some of the party organisation. He had just carried on wearing his habitual performance suit.

"Sorry," he said, "I was wondering how well our stake-out would work in this crowd."

She nodded. "I know. It's going to be a problem isn't it. I decided we needed more manpower, so, and don't be angry, I've let Bill and Alison in on the plan. So that's two more pairs of eyes watching."

And two more people to blow our cover, he thought. But he had to admit the task looked hopeless without help. Absently he kissed her forehead. Irene appeared through the crowd with her daughter in tow.

"John, thank you so much for letting Janice come. I couldn't have asked for yet more baby-sitting."

'Janice'. So that was the girl's name, he thought. Janice looked annoyed at the term 'baby-sitting', and said to her mother, "I don't need a child minder! I'm not a baby."

'Same name as Levi's secretary, I should be able to remember that.' He turned to the girl and, hoping to defuse the girl's annoyance at being treated childishly, asked, "Been watching the show?"

"Nah, I don't want to see it, it's Dickens. Why are you and that bloke," she nodded at Jimmy, "still dressed as penguins after the show's finished?"

Irene started to chide her daughter for daring to criticise the production and being rude, but John beat her to it with, "I know, Dickens is a real shame, but we have to put up with it. You'll enjoy this though. If I know anything about these sorts of after show things it'll be pretty lively."

"And probably quite unsuitably rude or even crude." the mother worried.

"Nothing worse than what gets said in the school dorm, I bet. Enjoy yourselves."

John and Lucy watched as the mother and daughter went further into the room.

"See if you can keep track of where they go," Lucy told him, "You're taller than me. Even if you are dressed as a penguin," she added grinning.

"Never insult the uniform," he told her, "and yes, they've gone over there... against the OP wall a couple of rows of tables back from the stage."

"Oh yes, I can see them now. Hey, why can't we sit with them, then we 'd be able to watch the girl all the time?"

"I think we need to leave room around her. In fact Irene is a bit of a nuisance really. No-one's going to make an approach with her mother in the next seat. Anyway it's only a two seat table."
Even as he spoke one of the cast appeared from behind the posters that were backing the temporary stage and went over to Irene. John could see a brief conversation. Irene exchanged a few words with her daughter, before rising and going 'backstage' with the cast member, leaving Janice on her own.

"What's happening?" Lucy wanted to know.

"I'm not sure, but I think Irene's just been press-ganged into the cabaret."

More people arrived. Some, like Lucy, had dressed for the occasion. A few had come very casually attired, including members of the local stage crew, in their stage blacks. The crowd was concentrated around the bar, but the rest of the room was very nearly full too.

Abruptly the lights dimmed and some of the temporary spotlights faded up, drawing everyone's attention to the stage. There were jocular 'Ooh's' from some of the crowd, and Oscar came out from behind the posters into the light. He went to the microphone, amid slightly ironic cheers, and tapped it, saying "Is this working?"

Laughter, and Robert, the sound engineer's voice from somewhere in the crowd shouting, "They always are!"

"Ladies, gentlemen and others who haven't made their minds up yet, welcome to this little soireé," more 'ooh's', "to celebrate 'Chuzzlwit's two hundred and fiftieth touring performance. Anthea tells me that she is starting to get the hang of the script now..." laughter... "and thinks we will be able to dispense with the prompter by the time we reach Newcastle," more laughs, "Meanwhile, as you might have expected, some of the cast have been making a few improvements to the lyrics for this evening's entertainment, so without further ado we bring you the opening number!"

There was applause, a lighting change, and some members of the chorus came on stage, joining the small group of musicians who had been setting themselves up behind Oscar's opening speech. They launched into a rendition of the show's opener, but with ribald words.

Lucy put her arm around John's waist and stood beside him hugging him and watching the cabaret. John scanned the crowd, not sure what he was looking for. So far as he could see the bulk of the attendees were watching the stage. Those who were not were at the bar or starting to graze at the groaning buffet tables. After a few sketches he told Lucy 'Wait here' and fought his way to the bar, returning with drinks for both of them. She took hers, and looked critically at the whisky he was holding, deducing, rightly, that it was a very generous double. He saw the look and said "Saves fighting back through the crush."

She shook her head slightly. "Don't drink too much, John."

"I'm fine," he answered, but she saw him gently rubbing the scar on his arm. She wondered if he was thinking of the dead actress, or whether, perhaps, something in one of the sketches had rung a bell from the original production. Out of the corner of her eye she saw Frank, doing a very believable impression of someone deeply involved with his partner, as he led Nicole through the room with his arm tucked into hers. Maybe that was what was upsetting John. She didn't know, so she cuddled up to him again as Oscar introduced another act, which turned out to be some of the male chorus with a frankly filthily worded send-up of one of the American sequence numbers. Her female intuition was partly correct, for John had seen Frank and Nicole too, and a pang of jealousy had him now wondering whether Frank needed to make the fake relationship quite so realistic. He could feel Lucy's possessive grip on his arm and suppressed a fleeting urge to shake her off and go across to Nicole.

Chapter 17

Elsewhere in the room Brenda and Alice had managed to get a position near the stage so they could sit looking back at the crowd. Despite this they too had realised that it was an almost impossible hope that any villain in the company would be evident in this gathering, even if they existed. In order not to lose their seats they took it in turns to go to the buffet and stock up on food. This operation took longer than expected, as aside from the crush they were each individually accosted by members of the company who wanted to say hello. The cabaret might be running, but many of the cast were seeing this as a social occasion, rather than a performance.

By the time Alice returned, to find Brenda half way through her plate of food, the whole room was very noisy. Near the front the throng was hurling back jibes at those performing whenever the act warranted it. In the middle of the party, mostly standing, were the people who were chatting, while watching the show with half an eye. Further back the eaters and drinkers candidly and steadily demolished the food, and ran up Levi's bar bill.

"Seen anything?" Alice said in Brenda's ear.

Brenda shook her head. "I can't even see the child through the crush," she said, her mouth right next to he colleage's ear, "but a couple of those musicians were being very cosy just now."

Alice turned slightly to look where Brenda had indicated. It was true. Two of the pit orchestra were deep in discussion, and as she watched one of them took something from his pocket and handed it to the other, who put it into his pocket without looking at it.

"What was that they passed?" she asked Brenda.

"Perhaps we've just seen a drugs deal."

"How can we prove it?"

"Did you learn any tricks from your pickpocket act?" she asked Alice.

"Well I used to do some of the lifts but people thought it was him 'cos everything ended up on the tray."

"So you can do it! Just go and take whatever it is out of his pocket then."

"I can't do that! What if I'm caught?"

"Alice this whole thing is a waste of time and money if we don't get some sort of evidence."

Alice looked at her boss very doubtfully. A loud round of applause drowned out any comment she might have made. Reluctantly she made her way across the room. She called at the bar and collected a fresh drink, returning close to the musicians. She contrived to collide with the one they suspected of having received something, slopping some of the drink onto him in the process. In the press of the crowd it was the most natural mishap. Brenda watched intently as Alice could be seen apologising, brushing the spillage off the musician, and coming away.

"Well?" asked Brenda when Alice arrived back.

Alice shook her head and held out her closed hand, then opened it to reveal a set of car keys.

"Oh great, now you've nicked his keys."

"Well I couldn't put them back! I guess they've decided one of them is the driver tonight and not drinking."

"We'll have to put them behind the bar and say we found them."

"I think someone else should 'find' them. Perhaps John...."

The two women looked about, trying to spot John, eventually catching sight of him, with Lucy still clinging to him, in the mêlée. John was clearly watching something, presumably looking for any suspicious activity, as they had all agreed to do. Lucy was tucked against his chest looking up at him, and certainly not keeping any sort of watch for villains. Neither of the wardrobe ladies could now see the child or Irene. They began to work their way to John. When they arrived Alice handed him the bunch of keys.

"You'll have to cover for me and say you found them on the floor," she finished her explanation.

John drained his glass, nodded, and said, "Wait here a minute, Lucy," disentangling himself from the girl and heading to the bar. Alice saw that on the way he stopped and bent down as if picking something up. When he rose again the keys were visible in his hand.

'He'd have made a good pickpocket's assistant,' she thought wryly.

John returned to Lucy from the bar, leaving the keys safely on a shelf, minded by the house staff, for the owner to reclaim. He was carrying drinks for both of them but looking around the room as he came. Lucy saw that the generous measure of before was now dwarfed by the half tumberful of whisky he held for himself.

"Oh John!" she said reproachfully, but he paid no attention and knocked a good portion of the drink back in one gulp.

The cabaret seemed to have come to an end, with a raucous chorus, and the crowd was starting to move about.

"Can you still see Janice?" Lucy asked.

"Yes, she's still there, but no-one's paying her any attention now," he said distractedly, scanning the party for a sign of Nicole.

"Let's go and talk to her and see if she'll tell us if anyone did speak to her."

They threaded through the throng. Janice sat rather glumly by herself.

"Did you enjoy the cabaret?" Lucy asked.

"All right I suppose,"

"Probably too many 'in' jokes," John said, "you needed someone to explain them to you I expect." He found himself shouting the tail end of this comment as someone set the sound system to playing current dance hits. "Didn't anyone come and offer?"

Janice shook her head. As she did so one of the chorus appeared, grabbed her by the wrist and said, "Come on, come and dance."

The girl resisted for a moment, but the floor was now starting to fill with members of the company dancing, or at least moving about, and she stood up and vanished into the scrum with the man.

"Edwin," Lucy told John.

"I know. And gay as a row of chiffon tents, so she's perfectly safe."

"Unless he's the dealer," Lucy said, "I mean why else would he come and drag a child onto the dance floor?"

"Maybe because he's just a nice bloke and he noticed she was bored and alone during the cabaret."

"We were with her now."

"All the more reason he might think that she needed rescuing."

Lucy thumped him and he came close to spilling the dregs of his drink.

Irene returned to where they were. "Where's Janice?" she asked, shouting above the din.

John and Lucy hadn't taken their eyes off the girl, "Over there dancing with Edwin."

"That's kind of him," Irene acknowledged. "I had to go and help them with the cabaret."

By unspoken mutual agreement John and Lucy gradually circled the room, keeping Janice in sight despite pausing to exchange a few words with cast and crew they met. A quarter of an hour or more passed, and the party was beginning to thin, before they saw Edwin steer Janice back to where Irene was sitting. Irene and Edwin exchanged a few words and he turned away.

"Well I didn't see him sell her anything, did you?" Lucy remarked.

"No, I think we may have been barking up the wrong tree there."

"Well if we were that was a waste of an evening."

"Let's wait till we've compared notes with the others," he said.

Eventually, when the party was all over, they left, and went back to the hotel, tired and a bit disappointed at not having had any concrete result from the event.

Lucy was summarising what they had managed to learn from the party as she sat on the edge of the bed, slowly taking off her shoes. Her hair hung down over her bare shouders as she bent forward to undo the buckles. John found he couldn't resist her, turned off the room's main light and went to kneel beside the bed next to her saying "The detecting can wait until morning," as he pulled back the bedclothes.

At about four o'clock in the morning he woke, as Lucy said loudly and with the clarity of someone who had not been asleep, "None of the kids' show people were there!"

"I saw Mark, their stage manager, and the girl who plays Mollie, what's her name?"

"Not Elaine and the rest though, perhaps no-one thought to invite them," she mused.

"I did."

"Perhaps it's good they ignored your invitation. There were enough people to try to watch as it was."

John grunted sleepily, put an arm round the girl, and pulled her back onto the pillows.

"I didn't see any drugs either," she said.

"Not the type we're supposed to be looking out for, no."

She stiffened slightly, surprised, and said "But....?"

"But there was some pot being smoked somewhere. Didn't you smell it?"

"I don't know what it smells like," After a pause she asked, "How do you?"

He shrugged. "If none of us really know what we are on the lookout for it could be a long search.. even if there is someone dealing."

Chapter 18

John hadn't really expected to be asked back to Bill and Alison's house again after the trauma of the raid, which he could not help but feel partly responsible for even though it had had nothing to do with him directly. However with just two more performance weeks at the Royal he found himself back there for another Sunday lunch.

This time, because his relationship with Lucy was established, and they were effectively living together, the two of them arrived at the front door hand in hand, although once drinks had been poured Lucy made off into the kitchen to help her sister in law.

Eddie was there again, but it was Emily who was dominating the conversation as they sat, glasses in hand, watching the child crawling around on the living room carpet with her dolls and cuddly toys. There was an anticipatory clattering from the kitchen, and a regular thumping noise outside as Bill junior satisfied his obsession by kicking a ball repeatedly at the fence.

"Did you like 'Chuzzlewit'?" John asked the girl, remembering that he hadn't seen her since he had arranged for comp tickets for the family to watch the show.

She looked up at him with bright eyes and nodded before returning to arranging her toys in a line.

"What did you like best?" Eddie prompted, turning a casual query into some sort of formal interrogation in the way that adults can do when talking to children.

Emily seemed to think for a moment before saying, "The costumes were very clean."

Both men laughed.

"It's not funny, it's very important!"

"You're quite right," John told her, "it is very important. What about the music?"

"I liked the songs I knew.." she paused, and briefly he thought she was about to start singing 'Come back love' again, "..and the ship. I liked the ship."

"I like that bit too," he told her, thinking of the opening of act two and the musical number, the dance routine and the life sized scenic piece that was the moveable ship. In a way he was surprised that the child, even one interested in scenic design, had noticed it enough to pick it out. It was one of those theatrical scenic tours-de-force that happened upstage of the main action. Once stage carpenters had prided themselves on producing the illusion of solidity from lightweight materials, now much of the scenery was frequently steel framed and consequentially weighty. The time was coming, he knew, when such brutally heavy and bulky pieces would be replaced by some form of projection. The audiences didn't know it yet, some of the managements didn't know it yet, but you couldn't work in the industry without being aware of the creeping advance of the electric departments over the old traditional skills. He wondered what those developments might mean for Emily's budding interest. He gave a mental shrug. She was only a child, her enthusiasm for settings would probably fade away.

"Are you coming to see my theatre?" Emily blurted out, jumping to her feet just as Alison came through the door from the kitchen.

"After dinner, Emily," she told her daughter, "Run outside and fetch your brother now... and wash your hands, both of you."

The family sat down in their places.

Another welcome, home made, meal, and through it all no-one made any comment on the police raid, or the damage it had caused. John and Lucy fielded a few questions about the show, but much of the conversation involved young Bill and his grandfather discussing football. John knew nothing, and cared less, about the sport and was grateful to be able to eat the meal while this chat went on.

"I'm sorry we didn't catch a dealer at the party," Alison said to Lucy.

"I'm not," said John, coming back to the present from whatever he had been thinking about, "it's just one more proof that there isn't one."

"What's a 'dealer', mummy?" asked Emily.

"Don't talk with you mouth full," said Alison.

"What's this about dealers?" queried her father "Have you found them?"

"Go on, tell him," John said, "We've drawn a blank anyway."

"The party the other night was to try to draw the supposed dealer out into the open so that dreadful woman would have to let us all off the hook. Bill and I went too so that John and Lucy would have as many eyes watching as possible," Alison explained, "It didn't work. Nothing happened."

"Which sadly proves exactly that.. nothing," John put in before Bill senior could begin to say that no news was good news.

Instead the older man said, "You'll never prove that something isn't happening. It's not possible."

John had had that very thought many times since Moira had disrupted all their lives. He said, "We're all open to suggestions."

Emily finished chewing and asked, "Is it like at cards, mummy?"

"Not quite," John told her, and to distract the child asked what her latest show in her toy theatre was going to be.

"It's a variety show, because 'riety and cabaret and vaudeville are best because people enjoy them. Some other plays and things are sad, so some people don't like them."

John wondered who'd been telling the girl that. It was so like his own view of styles and content that he wasn't sure if he'd said it to Emily last time he'd been at the house. On reflection he thought it more likely to have found its way into the child's thoughts from her Auntie Lucy, who could well have relayed the opinion from him. Anyway he probably wouldn't have told Emily about vaudeville, which might be thought a bit too risqué for an infant. She'd be better being directed to childrens' shows. Again his mind jumped back to 'Mollie's Garden'. Some comp tickets for that, next, he decided, making a mental note to enquire which day would be most convenient for Alison or Bill to take the girl.

Lucy could see him thinking. She had become increasingly aware of moments when John became deep in thought and wasn't really paying attention to the world around him. That was twice now during this meal. It was unlike him, for he was normally almost excessively aware of every detail of any show. Maybe he didn't extend this concentration into day to day life, she didn't know, because she had only ever really seen him in a work situation till recently. It worried her. She was certain that he was probably considering the difficulties of their amateur detective activities, but her own insecurities still made her wonder if he was thinking about Nicole. It was very unfair of Levi, she thought of him as Mr. Fischer, to impose Nicole on them. Lucy vaguely wondered if Levi had some ulterior motive in wanting his company manager to be reunited with Nicole. No, she told herself. That was silly. Perhaps she could confront him with the problem when he next put in an appearance. She was pretty sure he would come to the secret detectives' meeting tomorrow, after spending all that money. But she knew she would not confront him. It was normally unthinkable for a lowly wardrobe assistant to even speak to Levi Fischer, let alone question his judgement.

As a result of these concerns it was a pensive Lucy who was sitting on the floor of her neice's bedroom with John watching the child busily positioning those of her toys that were to star in the show on the model theatre stage. It was a big and impressive model theatre, occupying a good proportion of the girl's small room. The wooden stage and proscenium rose to a fly-tower that made the model nearly as tall as the child. This housed cords and screw eyes acting as pulleys, so scenery could be raised and lowered. There were deep red stage curtains that could be opened and closed by a string, and the arch they were mounted on was decorated in a copy of the ornate 'red-plush-and-gilt' style of the grand old theatres with fake pillars and comedy and tragedy masks above the centre of the arch. A selection of backdrops were flying above the stage and Emily chose one of these and put it in position at the rear of the scene.

She put a teddy against the proscenium arch facing onto the stage, and stood a doll centre stage, then she drew the bedroom window curtains.

"That's the houselights going out," she explained.

She pointed the torch that John had given her at the doll and started singing, holding the toy in her other hand and wiggling it in time to the tune.

She sang a currently popular number from the charts. Both John and Lucy vaguely knew the number from the repeated playing of it currently on radio stations. They both also had a slight idea that it was one of those numbers that stretched suggestiveness to the limits that would allow it airtime. It was called 'horizontal dancing'. Neither of them had previously heard it sung by a small child, especially a small child who clearly had no idea what it was about, and who's version included frequent misheard words, some of which moderated the rauchiness, many of which made it worse.

Lucy made as if to interrupt Emily, but John tightened his grip on her arm to restrain her, whispering in her ear, "She doesn't know what it means at the moment, but she soon will if you make her stop."

Lucy hesitated, then, after Emily had sung a few more lines, whispered to John, "I'm not sure a teddy could do that to a doll."

John bit his lip to control his laughter. Now viewed in that light the explicit requests of the song's vocals were risible when seeming to be a list of sexual desires from a plastic doll to a teddy bear.

Emily's show continued with less salacious content from then on. It was evident that she had absorbed the idea that a childrens' show could play 'underneath' a major show in the same venue, and she made a great feature of changing her scenery, some of which she had made herself so it was composed of bits of cardboard boxes painted in poster paints, when she announced that the second show was now to start. With the decisive insistance on things being exactly as she had decided in her mind that children often display the changeover was a bit of a drawn out affair. They watched as she sorted and re-arranged her cardboard settings, losing some essential part at one point,

"I can't find it! I can't find it!" the child protested in frustration, before finding it in an abandoned box.

"I knew I had it somewhere," Emily, suddenly calmed and happy again, told her aunt, "but I didn't know which box it was in."

The second show was rather bland, a version of Humpty-Dumpty, in which nothing much happened except that an old, multi-coloured, papier-maché Easter egg fell off an unstable brick wall rather too often. John and Lucy were not sorry when Alison's call from below brought the show to an end. They duly praised Emily, and went downstairs.

Later, as they walked back to the hotel, Lucy hugged his arm, looking up at him, and said, "You're very quiet."

"Just thinking about Emily's show."

"Thinking about being a bear and a doll tonight?" she teased saucilly.

"You wouldn't want to do those sort of things."

"How do you know," she let go of his arm and skipped ahead deliberately wriggling her hips flirtatiously, "why don't you come and find out?"

In John's mind a flash of recollection of Melanie, his first wife, was vivid and quite frightening. He remembered her violent lust and promiscuous behaviour. He didn't for a moment believe that Lucy was starting to behave like that, but something in her suggestive posturing, as she jokingly teased him, rang a bell. It annoyed him, bringing back the memories of his failed marriage.

"Don't do that," he said, more sharply than he had intended. Lucy stopped, allowing him to catch up with her, and walked alongside him, but separately, the light mood broken. At the hotel he made straight for the whisky bottle and poured himself a generous three fingers of spirit into a tumbler. He wiggled the bottle at her as a sort of peace offering, but she shook her head and said, "I wish you wouldn't either."

He ignored her ongoing concern at his increasing drinking. It helped to suppress the memory of Penelope, and that was good because the memory was painful. But he felt some guilt whenever he realised that a day, or even part of a day, had passed without thinking about her. He was confused. He wanted to remember her, he wanted to forget all about it. He rubbed the scar on his arm. Everything on this show seemed to be geared to taunt him with what he had lost in that crash. Levi's introduction of Nicole into the group to try to disprove drug smuggling. Even Lucy's little bit of raunchy put-on sexiness had brought up memories that all led to Penelope directly, or indirectly, for if the original production of 'Chuzzlewit' had run longer he would certainly not have been a part of that small scale theatre in education show. But then he might never have met Penelope.... and she'd still be alive.

He slumped onto the small settee and she came and knelt on the floor in front of him.

"What did I do wrong?" she asked.

Grudgingly he said, "It was too like Melanie."

"Your first wife?" She still knew very little of his earlier history other than what he had told her and a few hints from Brenda.

"Uh huh."

"Emily's bear and doll?"

"No, you acting up to it. It never actually crossed my mind while we were watching her show, but when you..."

"What were you thinking about then? You said you were thinking about Emily's show."

"I suppose so. Well no, not the show exactly, the scenery and the props."

"Oh trust you!"

"No really, I think we saw something important there, something to do with what we're supposed to be proving, but I can't put my finger on what."

That night he lay, wide awake, staring at the faint details of the ceiling, with its dated platerwork and ceiling rose, in the gloom, while Lucy slept deeply beside him. He, who could sleep in any circumstances, went over and over the day in his mind, trying to resolve what it was he had nearly realised just as Lucy had plunged him back into the past. It was something about Emily's show, but not the show itself.

Chapter 19

Monday came and they were now in the last week at the Royal. A busy weekend lay ahead once more. 'Mollie's Garden' would pull out on Friday, immediately after its matinee performance, then 'Chuzzlewit' would play Friday night and two shows Saturday before it too loaded its lorries and moved on.

John had no difficulties with comps for the Tuesday afternoon performance of 'Mollie'. For a kids show it was selling well, but the Royal's huge auditorium could easily accommodate the demand. Mark had no qualms about comps for John, cynically he needed to keep on the right side of him for future venues where 'Mollie' played under 'Chuzzlewit', but also because Lucy, who's costume modifications had been so well received, and for little Emily, the child of the owner of the company dealing with the costume laundry for them in this city. He told John to help himself, and Jimmy knew that the venue wasn't losing anything so he was happy to help out an old friend. Jimmy realised that John probably didn't want to watch the show, and was only sorting the seats for 'Auntie Lucy' and her niece. Even front of house was vaguely aware of the relationship between the wardrobe girl and the company manager that had blossomed during the run at the Royal. Jimmy took John's expressed preference for seats in hand, and the tickets they got from the box-office were end of row and several rows back from the front. John wanted to avoid a front row in case the show included any audience participation, which he disliked, though he hadn't told Lucy of this request to be further back.

John sat on the end of the row, with Emily between him and Lucy. The little girl was excited to be in the theatre again, though John, having considered 'Chuzzlewit' too grown up for her, thought she might be too old for 'Mollie's Garden'. He whispered his concern over the girl's head to Lucy.

"Nonsense," she said, "everyone loves 'Mollie's Garden.'"

He wondered whether this was true. He'd only ever heard of it because the stage show kept following him round the country. He couldn't recall the last time he watched afternoon television. He put his arm across the back of Emily's seat and laid his hand on Lucy's shoulder. Like this they appeared to be a perfect family group. The audience was noisy, chattering excitedly, and a collective 'Oooh' echoed across the auditorium as the play-in music ended and the houselights began to fade. In the darkness John was aware of the house tabs flying out. The stage lighting came up on the childishly colourful picturebook set and 'Mollie' burst onto the stage, waving excitedly to the children.

John looked down at Emily, noting that she was glued to the show. The cast worked enthusiastically in the heavy, bulky, costumes, each character dancing their own dance and singing their own song as 'Mollie' introduced her garden friends. John privately doubted a real Mollie, keen on flowers and growing things, would really be friends with a snail.

He sympathised with the cast, clad in the heavy sponge garments, trying to dance and sing. It struck him that in many ways the 'flowers' had the worst time, with fake leaves up to their waists or chests, and the flower head usually centred on the actor's face so the petals radiated out above, to either side, and below.

There was very little plot, the show being simply an excuse to introduce each of the characters already made famous by the TV show and to allow each of them to sing, or join in, a simple musical number. John wondered whether Emily was analysing the show in the same way he was so she could recreate the style on her toy stage.

After it finished, and the audience had clapped delightedly, he and Lucy took Emily home, stopping at a MacDonalds on the way, much to the child's glee.

"Say 'thank you' to auntie Lucy and...er.. uncle John" Alison told her daughter when they dropped her off.

Emily dutifully repeated the thanks, and then, impetuously hugged each of them in turn before saying, "Are you coming in to see my new show?"

They excused themselves, explaining that they had to go back to the theatre for the evening perfomance, and left. It was a fine afternoon and they walked, enjoying being together.

Lucy said, "That really wasn't your sort of show, was it? Thank you for coming."

John shrugged. "It entertained its audience. That's what really counts."

"I don't think I'd want to tour with it though," she said after they'd gone a few more paces, "Those little tunes would start going round and round in your head."

"Don't the 'Chuzzlewit' numbers?"

"Well yes, but you can force yourself into thinking about another one if one starts to irritate you. 'Mollie' numbers are all much the same. Whenever 'Come back love' sticks in my mind I try whistling 'Ergo ego'. At least that's a lively one."

He nodded. "We do lead very repetitive lives don't we? Same thing every day. Almost like working in a factory."

"You called it the 'fun factory' once."

"Yes." he thought for a moment while his mind went back to the on-going problem of the suspected drug transporting. "What puzzles me a bit," he said, rubbing his arm where the scar was itching, "is how, on a show like this, where everything is the same, week after week, venue after venue, you could expect to smuggle any moderate sized package, and I guess it must be, otherwise there'd be no point, into one of the trucks. We all know exactly what goes where, and what order it loads in."

"Do we? In that much detail?" Lucy was a bit disbelieving.

"Remember Tania's toolbox?"

"No." Lucy didn't come into contact with the deputy stage manger very much in the normal run of things.

"It was Truro, I think. The handle came off her toolbox, so during the time there she bought a new one. It didn't arrive in Sheffield on the Sunday. There was a big fuss. Our people didn't recognise the new box, so it got left on the Truro loading bay because everyone thought it must belong to one of the house crew. I had to send a cab for it."

"From Truro to Sheffield?" Lucy was shocked, "No, I didn't hear about that. Are we really that precise and organised on a get-out?" She thought about the wardrobe department's frantic acquisition of costumes as they were finished with on a last performance in a venue, the packing, and the way lots of stuff found its way out to waiting lorries even before the curtain fell.

"I hope so, otherwise there'd be bits of 'Chuzzlewit' scattered all over the country."

"Like Tania's toolbox," she teased him.

"Touché. The exception that proves the rule. The point I'm making is that either whatever the drugs travel in is constantly with the show.. in which case some department owns it and uses it, so either we're into a weird complicated world of false bottomed flight-cases, or a whole department is involved... or, I don't know," he ended lamely.

"Or 'Chuzzlewit' isn't the mule!"

"Oh aren't we getting into the lingo!" he laughed, "but you are right. The more I think about it the more I don't think it is."

Chapter 20

They met in wardrobe on Wednesday. Lucy was disappointed that Levi did not attend so she could question him about why Nicole had been asked to be involved, though she knew she would probably have been too over-awed to do any such thing. She came from a world where querying one's superiors had never really been encouraged. She assumed that John had already told the impressario all about the party, and explained that it had been a huge waste of money. If he had, he hadn't told her anything about that phone call or Levi's reaction. She wondered whether John was in trouble with his boss over the failure.

Wardrobe was crowded. When it was just Brenda, Alice and herself the room seemed quite spacious. Now they had been joined by John, Frank and Nicole. There was a shortage of chairs, and Lucy found herself sitting with John on the table that had been installed as a workbench for the show's touring costumiers.

John had been pensive at breakfast, only telling her, when she asked him, that he had remembered what it was that had struck him at Emily's 'show'. No amount of pressure would get him to say more and she found herself expecting a big revelation.

Frank and Nicole had arrived together and Lucy's female intuition was making her think that the pretence of a relationship had slipped into something more genuine. She tried to catch Brenda's eye, but the wardrobe mistress was concentrating her attention on John. Lucy turned her head to look at him, beside her, and saw that he, in turn, was fixedly studying the DSM and his ex girlfriend.

'He still fancies her,' Lucy thought sadly.

John started the meeting.

"Did everyone have a good time at the party?" There were affirmative murmurs. "You see, unfortunately, from what everyone has told me, we completely failed to flush out any villains, so I've had to explain to Levi that it was an expensive experiment that failed.

"So this is going to have to be a brain-storming session. Anyone got any ideas?"

There was some head-shaking. Brenda said, "I still don't believe there's anyone in the company peddling drugs."

"And that's where we have a real problem, because what we believe, and I think that we all agree, doesn't cut any ice with the boys in blue."

Frank said, "So who's got any suggestions then?" looking round the room. Various heads shook. Brenda said, "Surely every department knows what's happening among it's own members, I mean Alice and Lucy couldn't be up to no good without me knowing." She looked over to Lucy, gave a short laugh, and added, "Well I think I know what you are up to."

Lucy blushed and looked up at John beside her. He put an arm round her shoulders, and she cuddled closer to him in pleased surprise. Across the room Frank squeezed Nicole's hand and she gave a faint smile.

"So," Brenda went on, "All we need to do is check on each department in turn. I'll start with wardrobe. Here's a flat statement. No-one in wardrobe is pushing drugs."

"But it's still just our opinion, Brenda," said Frank, "I'm equally sure about all the stage people. The orchestra's a complete mystery, but I guess we could ask the fixer, but it still proves nothing. We can't prove a negative."

"Can we attack it from the other way round?" John said. "I can't see why anyone would bother to smuggle whatever drugs these are around the country on the back of a show, which they have no control over where it goes to. Wherever you have your store you could just pop the supplies for the street in the back of a car and drive to the street dealers whenever you liked. If you don't like the risk you send someone else, but car or bike is quicker, safer, less complicated and in your control."

The group thought about that for a second, till Frank said, "It must be Levi behind it then."

"Why do you say that?"

"Well ultimately he controls the tour schedule, where we go and when."

"But there'd still have to be someone in the company to handle the stuff," Alice pointed out.

"He does usually turn up at some venues after a get in weekend you know. But I'm sure it's not him. Look at the whole business of the party."

"It could have been a complicated and expensive camouflage, a double bluff," Alice suggested.

John felt that the discussion was now entering the realms of fantasy and getting away from him.

"The question now is 'who's going to challenge him?'" Alice continued, slightly flippantly.

"Look," he said, "Everybody, in every department, knows what gets put in what container to go on the lorries....."

"Except the orchestra, who pack their own instruments," Frank interrupted.

"Well, yes, I suppose you are right but... Anyway even they'd have to have a case big enough to take the instrument and whatever is being smuggled, to pack, and unpack the instrument somewhere away from the rest of the band in case they were seen, and somehow keep everything very clean, because, remember, the Old Bill had the dogs in at some point. I saw the van outside. If they'd found any trace it would have pointed the drug squad straight to whoever played the instrument in that case."

"Perhaps the muso takes the case away after the pit has been set up."

"Maybe. But someone would comment on them taking an 'empty' case off to their digs if they were seen." John rubbed his scar, "Anyway I can't imagine that there's enough space inside a muso's case, they are all fitted to the instrument."

"Except for drums cases," said Frank, warming to his theory.

"Oh yes, highly inconspicuous, walking out of the stage door with a drum case."

"It was just an idea," he said, annoyed.

"Are all these pushers on the streets, who the boys in blue think someone on the show is supplying, completely new to it. I mean is whoever it is creating new suppliers, or cashing in on existing ones?" Brenda wanted to know.

"Well they haven't told us anything much, but I get the impression that these are new dealers that appear once we've been in a particular town for a few days."

"So we've got ourselves someone who can go out into the highways and byways and find wannabe dealers, get a flight case or something shifted on and off one of our trucks under the noses of a whole department of the show without them noticing, and with no risk of anyone else opening that particular case, and can defeat the noses of the sniffer dogs? Pa! I don't believe it at all," said Brenda.

"Moira..." John started.

"Don't talk to us about her," said Brenda, firmly.

"She...," John pause, waited for another interruption, paused, found none came, and continued, "She was very nosy about boxes of washing powder.."

"Wasn't she just!"

"I gather it was because they came and went almost daily through the stage door, and I believe that she thought that the smell of the soap stopped the dogs from detecting anything."

"Does it?" Frank asked.

"I have no idea.." John started to say.

"Is that the only reason why she had them smash up my brother's house?" Lucy interrupted.

John nodded. "I think so," he could see she was upset at the recollection of what had happened, he held her shoulder reassuringly. He tried not to think about how he'd been told about Eddie's alleged gangster activities by Moira, Was it true? Did Lucy actually know about her father? Did Eddie's criminal interests include drugs? And, if so, was Lucy implicated? Could she really be carrying off an 'innocent victim' act so thoroughly, so well?

"..I've thought about the logistics, and, as I just said, the possibilities are very thin on the ground. A case which is familiar to the department it belongs to and the truck drivers, but is never opened, or at least only ever by one person and has enough space inside to hide a package.. oh yes, and is miraculously hermetically sealed so the sniffer dogs can't detect the contents. Unless...." he stopped. They all looked at him.

"Got it!"

There was a confused babble of 'well?' and "what?', and he said,
"It isn't us."

"I told you that," said Brenda.

"It's 'Mollie'"

"Why?" demanded Frank.

"'Mollie's Garden' plays under us, so it gets in after us. The sniffer
dog search didn't find anything, because 'Mollie' hadn't arrived
yet when they did it. The accusations have come about because
the new pushers have appeared just after we've rolled into town
for the past few cities, and 'Mollie' has followed us to all of
those."

"I bet a thousand random travelling salesmen have too if the Bill
bothered to check on them instead of victimising us," Alice put
in.

"Anyway, all the things you said about everyone knowing what's
in which flight-case with us would apply just the same to the
'Mollie' company, probably more so, because they're a smaller
crew," Brenda added.

"Except they've had a new ASM a few venues back, about when
the Bill is supposed to have become suspicious, and..."

"Has Justine left then?" Brenda wanted to know.

"I gather so. Her replacement is called Elaine. Cropped hair,
dungarees and badges..."

"Oh, I've seen her."

"Anyway at the same time as she joined them they had new radio mics, and the old radio mic case is still with them, but, obviously, no-one needs to open it, it's just travelling around with them. Except... I bet that was the case I saw her leaving here with a few days ago."

"I think you've simply found a loophole that would make it possible. You haven't proven anything. Possible isn't the same as proof," Brenda said doubtfully.

"The police will think it's the same," Alice said.

"I reckon you've solved it," Nicole was supportive. Frank looked at her beside him with a rather suspicious expression, and Lucy raised an eybrow at the actress' eagerness to accept John's hypothesis. 'She might be cosying up to Frank,' she thought, 'but that torch she is still carrying for John shows though every so often.'

"If the drugs are supposed to be travelling on the lorries from city to city, why don't they bring in the dogs to stand by the loading ramps on a get-in or get-out?" Frank wanted to know.

"They'd lose the chance to nick someone actually in possession wouldn't they? I mean when we're loading in and out there are dozens of pairs of hands, both ours and the venue's, moving all the flight cases about. How do you prove that the crew member shoving a particular case along has any connection with its contents?"

John nodded thoughtfully.

"I think we pass the suggestion on to Levi, and let him convince the authorities. Let them decide what to do. But I'm convinced. I got that it had to be some sort of container always travelling with the show, but it wasn't until Emily couldn't find something she wanted for her toy theatre that I remembered how thoroughly we all know where everything is. It had to be a case no-one had any use for. It has to be 'Mollie's old radio mic case."

"....and that must be the case I saw her carrying out of the stage door when I came in just before the party." said Nicole.

Chapter 21

Nicole was grateful for Frank's supportive closeness. She wouldn't normally have spoken up like that without being asked a direct question, but she was becoming more comfortable in the presence of the 'Chuzzlewit' crew, and, overridingly, she still wanted to support John and his theory loyally. She hoped that the group would pass his opinion to Levi, and that hope brought a thought to her mind that if she could get to speak to Levi again she might be able to remind him of his promise of work for her.

She had become inceasingly worried that Laurence, who had only phoned once since he left for town, and had presumably drifted away into the London theatre world, never to return to her, would soon stop paying for the flat and make her move out. The call had been purely to check if there had been any mail. She had been conscientiously forwarding his post, and the bills, to him care-of the stage door, as she hadn't been given any other contact address. Recollections of the era of unsatisfactory digs and penny pinching meals nagged at her in moments when she was alone and unoccupied. She and Frank were both enjoying their relationship, which was now well beyond the fake cover it had started as, but she was uncertain what would happen at the end of this week when 'Chuzzlewit' pulled out of town and made its way to another theatre. She thought it unlikely that Frank would invite her into his accomodation in the next city in the way that John had done way back, when they were both with Theatre Wagon.

Spurred on by wishing to make contact with Levi on her own account she suddenly blurted out, "I'll ring Mr Fischer and tell him if you like."

Frank's eyebrows raised very slightly. Like John before him he had become aclimatised to, and fond of, Nicole's un-demonstrative reserve. It was unlike her to push herself forward. There were shrugs all round. Lucy felt that Nicole's motives were those of someone transparently supporting John's deductions. Brenda and Alice were unconvinced too, but happy to pass the buck indirectly back to Levi.

So it was agreed that Nicole would speak to Levi.

Within an hour she had rung his office, and, despite a little resistance from Janice, had been connected to the impressario.

"And also, Mr Fischer," she said, gabbling slightly from the urgency of her request, "you did say that you'd try to find me some position on a show.... now this investigating the drug running has been sorted out."

"Quite right, Miss Wade," Levi dropped into the expansive mode of speech he used when bestowing some sort of praise on an employee, "I have a sit-com about to go into rehearsal that needs an acting ASM. Would that suit?"

Levi knew that whatever he had offered to Nicole would have 'suited', and by the time she hung up she had written down dates and places, and agreed to be at some provincial rehearsal rooms in a few days time.

"What's the acting ASM's part?" she asked him.

"It's a nice little role," he assured her, "It's a neighbour who comes round to complain about the noise and ends up locked in a bedroom. All the usual comedy misunderstandings."

'All the usual running about from one door to another in your underwear' he thought to himself, but didn't tell her.

She was so relieved and excited by the prospect of working again, on a show which was already booked for a thirteen week tour of fairly large venues, that she was able to forget all about the suspected drug running. She was sorry to be leaving Frank's side, for it had been a comfortable, if brief, affair. She was sorrier still to separate from John once more. But the idea that her career was finally on a safe footing again for at least a quarter of a year was warming.

Levi made several phone calls to set up Nicole's new job, to check on some legal points with his solicitors, and then finally to the police.

John was in a quandry as to whether to forewarn Mark. He was certain that 'Mollie's' stage manager was entirely unconnected with any dealing that might have been going on. He convinced himself that the blame must lie with the new ASM. Reluctantly he restrained himself from saying anything, even when he and Mark were having a drink together in the pub. They chatted a bit about the arrangements for 'Mollie's' get out. John thought it was possible that the police wouldn't be letting things run quite as smoothly as the two of them envisaged.

The last performance of 'Mollie's Garden' finished, as always, amid enthusiastic, young, applause.

'Mollie's' cast trudged to their dressing rooms, shedding bits of the bulky costumes and handing in radio mics as they passed. On their way up the stairs the heavy suits were mostly being taken off and the actors and actresses were revealed hot and sweaty in their underwear as they reached their rooms.

John and Lucy watched the 'Mollie' cast passing the end of the wardrobe corridor on their way upstairs.

"I won't be sorry to see the back of those costumes," Lucy told him.

"Your brother will miss the extra income," said John.

"I don't think he'll really be sorry to see 'Chuzzlewit' leave the town either," Lucy told him.

"No, I suppose that's understandable."

"John, how are you getting to the next place?"

"I sometimes hitch a lift in Reg's truck, but.. If you're sharing my hotel room again," he raised an eybrow and she nodded, "we ought to go together for convenience."

"I'll get Daddy to arrange a car."

"Really?"

"Oh yes, he likes you, and he owns some car hire firms."

"Oh. Need to be careful with the drinking then."

"No, no. He'll send a driver. But I wish you would be careful with the drinking anyway."

"It just helps a bit, to soften the pain, you know."

She took his hand and looked at his scar.

"That's not all that hurts," he admitted

She raised her head and saw the tears starting in his eyes. Impulsively she put her arms round him and hugged him fiercely.

"I know I'm not her, but I do love you."

'Which 'her' do I mean? She thought as she said it.

He patted her and turned away in embarassment at having shown his emotions. He went into his office abruptly, and although he didn't shut the door to stop her following she knew he didn't want her with him at that moment. She went to wardrobe.

John sat at the makeshift desk and thought.

He was still there, with the casting directory open in front of him at the usual page, when the quiet background noise from the turned down show-relay speaker on the wall changed from the gentle clatter of 'Mollie's Garden' being struck and loaded to a series of authorititive shouts. He deduced that the police had arrived. He turned the volume up a little, and was unsurprised to catch raised, commanding, voices domineering a background counterpoint of surprised protest from the resident crew members.

Sadly he got up and found a bottle, pouring whisky into a used coffee mug before knocking it back in one, putting the mug aside, and making his way out into the corridor. Several people had appeared, and the effect was of a small crowd gathering curiously at the scene of an accident. He shouldered his way to the stage door, using the stairs as the lift seemed not to be moving.

Members of the 'Mollie' company were being led out by uniformed police in bulletproof vests and festooned with belts loaded with bulging pouches and radios.

Moira appeared in the midst of the fray, similarly clad, her face set in a hard mask of determination.

"You don't need to be arresting everyone, you know," he said to her when he was within earshot, "You were told who it was."

"They'll be released without charge if they can prove it's nothing to do with them," she snapped, "I'd stay out of this if I were you."

"That's not how the law works in this country," he remonstrated, "you have to do the proving, not them, and the cast are not involved."

"I said 'stay out of it'" Moira told him, but her boss arrived at that moment. John decided there was a chance that he might be able to curb the woman's worst excesses, and he went back up to the office.

Chapter 22

The news spread round the 'Chuzzlewit' company. Many people who had been unaware of what had been going on 'behind the scenes' now announced that they'd known all along that something was happening.

The Royal's front of house curtain rose on the Friday evening performance of 'Chuzzlewit' with a happier and somehow relieved cast and crew. During the second half Mark knocked on John's door.

"Mark," John said, "I'm really sorry you got embroiled in all that."

"So am I." He looked at the bottle behind John. John picked it up and said, "Want one?"

"I think I deserve one."

They sat in silence for a few moments, drinking the spirit. Then Mark said, "I wish you'd tipped me the wink, I mean I could have made some preparations. I'm going to have a right time of it next week with no other staff on stage management."

"We were under very strict instructions not to let anyone know... I guess you heard about all the trouble we had when that Moira woman got it into her head that 'Chuzzlewit' was the source of the supply?" He rubbed his scar.

Mark asked, "How did you get that scar?"

John hadn't had to explain his history to an outsider for so long that he was at a loss.

"There was an accident. The truck with the set in ran off the road."

193

"Was anyone else hurt?"

John thought, 'He really doesn't know.' and said, "One of the actresses was killed."

The silence prompted John. Suddenly he had to explain to Mark all about the small scale show, himself and Nicole, and then Penelope, and the crash. He poured more drink as he told him. It was curiously liberating. After all the months of avoiding talking about it, months of bottling it up, he unburdened himself to a casual acquaintance. He didn't burst into tears or moan about what had happened, he told it simply and straightforwardly. But he poured more drink as the account went on even though Mark kept putting his hand over his glass in a gesture of 'no more'.

As the level of the bottle went down the talk turned to show business and theatres, at least John talked and Mark, mildly shocked by the revelations, listened. John started to expound on one of his favourite theatre subjects.

"The modern architects know nothing," he said, "They've got no feel. No feel. All they're interested in is Health and Safety, bloody Health and Safety. No soul, no feel. That's what it is, no feel. Places like this," he encompassed the theatre they sat in with a wide sweeping gesture, "they're alive. They make you want to go in and enjoy yourself. Feel." he paused momentarily to take a gulp of his whisky.

"You don't get 'feel' with modern theatres. It's all clinical, all safe, no feel.
"You take a show into a proper theatre, like The Royal for example, and you know the house will feel right. You know what I mean, you've been in a few. You go into one of these modern monstrosities, 'The Blackborough Civic', 'The Billingsbury Playhouse', and it's all safety this and safety that and to hell with entertainment."

When Mark eventually left and John was alone in the office he drained the last of the bottle and decided that the catharsis he had just had was entirely made possible by what he had drunk. Now he was sure he knew how to deal with the bouts of misery.

He could hear the end of the show approaching. He tidied the desk with the concentrated care of the slightly inebriated and set off to find Lucy.

End of performance chores finished they headed back to the hotel.

"I told Daddy to get us a car for about three o'clock, but he won't mind waiting."

He groaned inwardly. He loved the business, but in his present mood he didn't relish another show get-out to the early hours, followed by travel, with only the promise of an arduous couple of days as the show settled into its new venue. He worried about Lucy. Waiting for him to finish would mean she was much later escaping than need have been the case. Wardobe had an enviable reputation for being among the first out of the building on get-out nights. An image of Penelope waiting patiently for him on that dreadful night crossed his mind.

He remembered her sitting in the stalls and watching as the show came to pieces and was stacked against a wall ready for loading. watching as a bars flew in and were de-rigged. She had watched as the wardrobe skips and rails came through from the dressing rooms and were stood by the dock door.

He remembered seeing Penelope shiver as the night air came into the theatre when the scene dock doors were opened, displacing the warm fug of the building's recently departed audience.

"Say something," Lucy prompted him, "What are you thinking about?"

"Sorry, I was just thinking about tomorrow's get out. It's going to be all of three before it's finished. Will you mind waiting?”

“No. Daddy's told his driver it might be later than that.”

“Not the driver... you.”

“Of course I don't mind. I'm happy to wait for you.”

Chapter 23

The typical Saturday in a touring show's routine was only slightly disturbed by Levi's telegrams. One addressed to John read:- 'Congratulations on outcome. See you later in tour. Levi' The other, addressed to the whole company, and pinned to the backstage noticeboard read:- 'Never doubted you all. Proud of how you carried on. Well done. Break many more legs. Fischer'

The company was pleased by a message from Levi at this late stage of the tour. John wondered how much 'later in the tour' Levi would put in an appearance, and why he was continuing to be so nocicably absent. 'Perhaps he has some new project brewing' he thought. He was frustrated at not being able to talk this over with anyone on the show. Brenda was happy at the eventual outcome of the 'investigation' but still seemed to be watching him, and his relationship with Lucy, very closely. Frank had turned rather cold on discovering that Nicole was being taken away to another of Levi's shows. He seemed to blame John, though in truth John had not pushed her case very hard and now felt guilty about that. And Lucy...

Now John felt great concern for the girl's welfare. As time went on he was realising that he was not 'getting over' Penelope's death, and that, despite that, he still felt a twinge of jealousy at Frank and Nicole's relationship. Drink was a solution, and he was depending on it more and more.

Packing up his office he loaded paperwork into cases. The copy of 'Spotlight' was the last thing to be packed. He rubbed the scar on is arm, staring down at the volume. Then, decisively, he closed the lid and locked it.

Like any get out the scenery, sound, lighting and props were stripped from the venue swiftly and efficiently by the crew, and loaded into the waiting lorries. Reg had spoken to John only briefly during the afternoon. He had obviously heard all about the police, and the lorry drivers' grapevine was full of stories about how disruptive the search of the 'Mollie's Garden' lorry had been. Discreetly he only said, "At least you've got rid of that Moira woman."

True to her word Lucy was sitting in row 'C' in the stalls when they finally came to the end of the loading process. The stage was empty, though big balls of grey fluff, built up on ledges over the weeks of residence and now disturbed, blew around on the floor in the draught from the loading bay. She came down the gangway and through the pass door to join John who was involved in the handshakes and 'goodbyes' of departure.

The car was waiting outside for them. It was a big black limousine driven by a muscular man in a black suit. There was, John thought, definitely something gangsterish about the overall style, but he welcomed the quiet comfort of the rear seats and even failed to be annoyed at the failure of the driver to join in his attempts at conversation.

Lucy cuddled close to him on the back seat as they sped off through the dark city streets toward the next venue. They exchanged a few murmured sentences before she fell asleep on his shoulder. John tried to stay awake, concentrating on watching the road through what he could see of the windscreen, and reminded of the winding country road and of him and Penelope in the truck together. But soon he too slept.

* * *

In the grey light of the next morning a wardrobe girl and a company manager were among the few members of the 'Chuzzlewit' crew who had had a night's sleep, however short that might have been.

As the lorries off-loaded and the backstage show-relay speakers vibrated to the irregular crashings and bangings of heavy scenery being moved and assembled John settled into his new company office. It was more plush than the last one as it was dedicated to this specific purpose and not a dressing room doubling as an office. He opened the first case of paperwork and took out 'Spotlight'. He hardly needed the bookmark to find the page as the volume almost fell open at Penelope's picture. He put the book in the middle of the desk and stood looking at it. Lucy burst in with hardly a knock saying, "Brenda says can you get someone to sort out the washing machine power....." She stopped seeing the book and John studying it. "Oh!" she said. Then angrily she said, "When you've got time!" and left, slamming the door.

John shut the book. Found the bottles. Took a good long fortifying swig as a substitute for breakfast and went out into the backstage world to find a house electrician to wire up Brenda's washing machines.

* * *

That night John and Lucy had a furious argument. They were both conscious of neighbouring hotel guests, so the row was conducted in vicious whispers.

"I can't go on with you constantly thinking about that actress," Lucy told him.

"Look, I can't help it if I think about her..."

"Yes you can! You can stop looking at her picture for a start."

"It's not something you can just turn off..."

"And you've been drinking again. Even on a get-in day! When everyone else is working their butts off you get to moon over some ex, and drink yourself stupid."

"I haven't drunk that much, and she's not just an 'ex' or 'some actress', she had a name, she was called Penelope, and... Who the hell is that?" he broke off at a knocking at the door.

199

He opened the room door angrily. Frank stood on the threshold with Nicole behind him.

"Bad moment?" asked Frank.

"Er, no, no, we were just...."

"I think I'm going to make it worse," Frank said, sympathetically.

John looked at him quizzically. Behind him, in the room, Lucy was wiping her eyes, for the girl had realised that this was probably the end.

"You'd better come in."

The double room seemed crowded now, Frank and Nicole ignored the vague gesture towards chairs that John made, and Frank said, "Nicole travelled up here with me last night, she's leaving to join the play that Levi's cast her in, right now, but she wanted to say 'goodbye' to you."

Nicole and John looked at each other for a long moment, until Nicole went to him and hugged him, whispering in is ear, "Oh John, I'm so sorry!" He could feel the slim body he remembered through the same smart, straight, camel coloured coat she had worn before.

Lucy watched. John had a desperate moment when he wanted to kiss the actress, but he simply patted her gently on the back and said, "Break a leg," before letting go of her. She went back to Frank's side.

Frank had been watching too. Now he said, "I've had a word with Levi, and he's agreed to put me on the same show as Nicole. He's moving the stage manager of that show across to 'Chuzzlewit' immediately. I'll work the first week here alongside him... show him the ropes.. a bit of a jump from a play to a major musical for him, but Levi seems confident enough, and then I'll be with the sit-com thing for the last two weeks of its rehearsals."

"You've got it all worked out then," John said bitterly.

"Levi said he would tell you, but I wanted to let you know myself."

"Thank you, I suppose."

Lucy said, "Oh Frank, we'll all miss you, but I hope you and Nicole will be very happy."

Frenk and Nicole held hands, looked at each other, and Frank said, "Oh I think we will."

Nicole looked back toward John, and he saw the same expression on her face that she'd had on that day when Laurence had collected her from John's hotel when they'd all been touring that little show all that time ago. It was a look that said 'I'm happy to be leaving with him, but I do so wish I could have stayed with you."

The visitors departed. John and Lucy, alone again, were quiet, both wondering how to restart their 'discussion', both conscious of the change this news might bring to their relationships.

Eventually Lucy broke the silence.

"Brenda told me to say I couldn't put up with you wanting Nicole, but I suppose that problem's been solved. Maybe I could have accepted being in competition with a live 'ex', but I can't cope with being in competition with a dead one too."

"I can't just turn it off you know. Anyway what do you mean 'Brenda said'?"

"We talked," she said.

"Why didn't you talk to me?" he asked sadly.

"I did, you know I did. I've asked you over and over again to stop drinking so much, and you know your exes upset me. Call it insecurity if you like, say I'm selfish, but I just can't do it..."

"Lucy, I really like you, care for you. I can't help it if I've got a past. At my age it would be weird if I didn't have. You've just seen Nicole go off with Frank... that's the second time she's ditched me. I've got a right to be a bit upset."

"And Penelope?"

"If I hadn't been so unkind to her at the start of that tour, well if her car hadn't broken down. Lucy, she should never have been in that scenery truck with me in the first place. OK, the courts were quite clear it wasn't my fault, but I can't help feeling responsible. And I did really love her you know."

"If, if, if!" Lucy said softly, "Well here's mine. If I hadn't fallen for you, if you weren't still in love with Nicole, if you weren't constantly thinking about Penelope and if you didn't keep drinking!"

He stopped, midway through reaching into the hotel room's mini-bar.

"I'm sorry, John," she said, and her lip trembled as she added, "We are finished."

The next day he went to see Brenda. He found her alone in the wardrobe, both Alice and Lucy were around the dressing rooms somewhere distributing costumes. Brenda greeted him rather coldly.

"Brenda, I think you at least owe me an explanation. What ever did you say to Lucy?"

"She was upset. You upset her. I just gave her some motherly advice."

"You told her to break it off with me?"

"Yes, I told her to finish with you. It wasn't fair on her. And yes, she's upset. We hardly need the washing machines any more, we just let her cry onto the costumes."

"What about me, Brenda?" he asked the wardrobe mistress, "Did you think about me being upset?"

"Yes, I did. I thought it might jolt you out of your self-centred moping and drinking."

* * *

There was no director's suite for Levi Fisher to recline in at this venue, but he had borrowed the front of house mnager's office and was comfortably installed behind the desk, swinging the swivel chair back and forth gently, his large frame overflowing the sides of the seat, a half smoked cigar clutched in his fingers.
"As there's been some shuffling of roles and replacement of personnel on the 'Chuzzlewit' company I have decided to make all the changes more or less at once."

'Who's for the chop now?' John thought to himself, facing the entrepreneur across the desk.

"I've got a new show starting to go into production. It's a big musical, and it's going to be a huge hit, so I've got 'Fessle and Northwich' on board." John raised an eyebrow. It was very unlike Levi to share any show with another production company. This must be a very high budget thing. "The usual routine, rehearsals, then a pre London tour. Some of the music is getting recorded for release as a single as we speak. I want you to be the company manager for the tour, and in the West End when it reaches there."

"What about 'Chuzzlewit'?"

"I'm moving you off it so you can start on this new show at once. Oh don't worry, I've got a couple of people to step in."

"I might not want to leave 'Chuzzlewit', Levi," he said, "And you know I don't like disturbing the established set-up."

"John, my boy, believe me, you do want to leave it. You had a bad time with it first time round with that dancer, this time round you've got involved with a wardrobe girl and upset the wardrobe department.. and we can never have that." He gave a short laugh to prove he was joking, but only partly. "Remember, my boy, I trust you with my investments."

John nodded sadly. Only three days into the latest venue and strained relations with Brenda and her staff were obvious, if only in limiting the number of places he could go for a cup of coffee. Still there were other things to drink besides coffee.

"What's the show?" he asked.

"It's going to be a real smash. It's a musical version of a very old plot, 'Faustus!'"

Also by Cliff Dix

*Theatre Wagon
And Burnt The Topless Towers
and
Up The Fire Escape And Through The Kitchens*